THE
LILAC
GARLAND

THE LILAC GARLAND

Nancy Richards-Akers

Thorndike Press • Thorndike, Maine

Library of Congress Cataloging in Publication Data:

Richards-Akers, Nancy.
    The lilac garland / Nancy Richards-Akers.
        p. cm.
    ISBN 1-56054-013-3 (alk. paper : lg. print)
    1. Large type books. I. Title.
[PS3568.I314L55   1990]   90-35647
813'.54--dc20   CIP

Thorndike Press Large Print edition published in 1990 by
arrangement with Warner Books.

Cover design by James B. Murray.

The tree indicum is a trademark of Thorndike Press.

This book is printed on acid-free, high opacity paper. ∞

This book is dedicated to the memory of Lois Akers Clark, an ardent romance reader, who introduced me to the splendid world of romantic fiction, and a lady who was a genuinely spunky and strong-willed heroine in her own right.

One

Winter's End, 1817.

Dame Fortune was smiling on Edward Latham, the Right Honorable Lord Tweeddale. This was the third hand of loo that evening, and Lord Tweeddale, known to his better friends as Ned, had just been dealt the jack of clubs. Without betraying the slightest hint of delight, he tilted the cards toward his chest, then lounged against the back of the armchair. From the corridor the peal of a clock striking drifted into the card room. Lord Tweeddale allowed the timepiece to complete the eleventh chime before casting a sideways glance at the dark-haired man seated next to him.

"You say you're going to Park Village East on business, Ramsey? Can't fathom anything so pressing to require your presence in that nouveau enclave of bourgeoisie commoners," he disdained. The recently constructed villas in Regent's Park had a fashionable enough address to escape Tweeddale's scorn, but

Park Village East, the quarter designed for the monied working class, was another matter entirely. "The neighborhood's inhabited exclusively by merchants, mostly tenant farmers and day laborers who've made their way out of the fields and into trade. Not the sort of people you ought to mix with for any purpose."

At this, Duncan Ramsey, the Earl of Croick, who had been arranging his hand of cards, set them facedown on the leather-topped table. He regarded his friend with his piercing blue eyes. "Hadn't thought of it that way, Ned. Doesn't make any difference though, for I do intend to visit Park Village," he said, his deep Highland brogue resounding with conviction.

"The rumors are true then?" inquired the third man who sat with them at White's. He was Christopher Jessup, Viscount Durham, the last member of the trio who had been friends since they boarded together in College House while attending Harrow. And this was Tuesday. The three men always met at White's on Tuesdays for dinner and an evening of cards when they were in Town. Tonight they had dined on turtle soup, salmon and turbot, a baron of beef with new potatoes, and gooseberry tartlets. The game was three-handed loo, jack of clubs high, and the stakes were moderate at a crown a point.

"Rumors?" queried Tweeddale. His eyes glinted at the prospect of tattle that might feature someone other than himself as the main player. "Go on, Durham," he urged. A wicked smile touched his lips. "Do tell all."

The viscount discarded a nine of diamonds, took the trick and without shifting his gaze from the game, he said, "Heard Ramsey's got charge of a female relative."

At mention of Ramsey's name in connection with a female, Tweeddale exclaimed, "Devil a bit! Hope you don't plan to back out on my sister. Announcement's already appeared in the paper. Not honorable to beg off, y'know. Not honorable atall."

"Hardly that, Ned. My man of business merely informs me that along with my uncle's title and lands, it appears I've inherited responsibility for a distant cousin." Ramsey picked up a brandy snifter and idly twirled its crystal stem between two long, bronzed fingers. With intentional deliberateness, he revealed, "Appears this relation is a single lady living on her own resources."

This tidbit of intelligence captured Tweeddale's interest. "An unattached female with her own funds, you say. Don't know her, do I? Plan to get her settled?"

"Egad, no!" Ramsey responded, not looking up from the leather-topped table. He discarded the queen of hearts and looed Tweeddale, who was loath to part with his jack so early in the game.

"She's a veritable antidote," struck in Durham. Of the three, the viscount was the only one who was married and thus privy to the tattle bantered about the drawing rooms of Mayfair. "Heard from Olivia that the gabblemongers say the lady's been living on an old estate of the family at the edge of the park 'cause she never took. Her Season was a disaster. Something about love scorned and can't bear to face the beau monde. Don't tell me you're interested in her, Ned. Even *you* can't be that desperate."

Lord Tweeddale colored as he downed a healthy swill of brandy. He stared intently at the table while Ramsey went on:

"Having never met Lady Christina, I can only surmise the description is an accurate one. From everything my solicitors say, she's likely strong-willed into the bargain as well. Certainly not the wife for our Ned. Eh, Durham?"

"I should think," mused the viscount, tossing Ramsey a wink, "that variety of wife generally runs a household like a military campaign. Remember Athelstane down at Harrow? Married an heiress and poor chap's been run ragged since. Stringent rules and all that."

"And a sorrier fellow there ain't," declared Ramsey. He took the next trick and drew another card. Soberly, he added, "No doubt Lady Christina would have Ned keeping regular hours, drinking a dish of tea with every meal, and banking his money in nothing but the most sensible investments."

The object of their amiable jesting shuddered.

Ramsey relented. "Don't go into the fidgets, Ned. You're quite safe. Lady Christina's likely prodigiously content with her husbandless condition. Most spinsters are, I collect."

"If not marriage, then what do you intend with the old girl?"

"Can't but do the civil," Ramsey responded. "Thought I'd call on her and see how she's faring. Must get boring, being on her own all the time. P'raps I'll suggest she join my household as a companion to Penelope."

"Capital notion. My sister'd like that immensely." Tweeddale gave an approving nod.

"You're taking this inheritance dead seriously," Durham observed silkily. He raised an ornate quizzing glass to take a long hard stare at his friend. Duncan Ramsey did not appear any different than he had the last time the friends had met at White's the previous summer. He was as darkly handsome as he had always been; his sharp chiseled face, framed by thick black hair, was offset by exquisitely starched shirt points, their pristine whiteness heightening his irrefutable masculine aura. Duncan Ramsey was a sportsman, an athlete, and a soldier whose crisp blue eyes surveyed a crowded room with uncanny skill. An elegant gold-tipped cane, his sole concession to the painful stiffness in his left leg, was propped against one lean thigh. Owing to the military genius of General H. Shrapnel, Ramsey had received a near crippling wound three years ago when one of the general's newly invented shells exploded outside his tent during his service on the Peninsula.

In every way he resembled the carefree rake who had won as many hearts as there were stars in the sky. He still smiled in that same, slightly cynical fashion, one dark brow arching in counterpoint to the curl of his full mouth. But looks were not everything, and there was no denying that Ramsey was acting deucedly strange.

It was less than a year since Captain Duncan Ramsey had been elevated to the rank of earl, as his paternal uncle's heir to vast holdings northwest of Inverness in the Scottish

Highlands. And it was but three weeks since he had returned from the north to embark on the mission of finding a wife. The purpose of his visit to London had rendered his friends speechless, particularly given the speed with which he had accomplished the task, managing to betroth himself to the Honorable Penelope Latham before a fortnight had elapsed.

"Hardly seem to know you these days," remarked Durham. "Still can't credit the notion of your getting leg shackled to Ned's baby sister."

"Nothing wrong with my sister."

"Didn't mean to imply there was. Olivia's quite fond of the chit. Sweet as a damson cake and retiring as a schoolroom miss, she says, and that's the rub. Penelope ain't your usual sort of female, atall, Ramsey."

"And why not? I want a wife, not a mistress," the earl rejoined. "Penelope's a pretty little thing, soft-spoken and in possession of a kindhearted, generous nature. I'm sure I couldn't want for a more perfect wife."

"That's all?" Durham wanted to know. "There's nothing else between you?"

"Egad, what else could there be? This isn't a love match, you know," said Ramsey.

"Ah, *l'amour*," drawled Tweeddale. " 'Tis so unfashionable. So bourgeoisie." He took out his snuffbox and helped himself to a liberal pinch.

Ramsey elaborated, "I must carry on the line, and I intend to do it sooner rather than later. I'm seven-and-twenty, and one lonely winter at Lochincairn was sufficient penance for anything I may have done in my youth. I don't intend to return north without a wife."

What he did not say aloud was that once he had cared for something more in a wife, but the only lady who had struck his fancy had turned him down last summer. Having declared that she could marry only for love, Miss Mina O'Kieffe had refused his offer and married the Earl of Brierly. Her choice was evidence of the sort of independent spirit he admired; the Countess of Brierly, née Mina O'Kieffe, was an uncommon woman, and Ramsey thought it distinctly unlikely that he would ever encounter so thoughtful and lively a lady twice in a lifetime. All that remained was to find an agreeable female, and Ned Latham's sister, Penelope, was a suitable enough choice.

"Lochincairn does sound fair grim," the viscount allowed. "And it's clear you must find a wife someday, but taking in spinster relatives is another matter entirely. Next we'll hear you fancy not just an heir, but a full nursery of squalling infants."

"And what's wrong with that? Now that you mention it, I believe I fancy the notion of a house full of children," came the startling revelation to which both the baron and the viscount responded as if struck dumb by a thunderbolt. Observing their disbelief, he emphasized, "Well, I would. Had you thought you'd be the only one of us to experience matrimonial bliss, Durham? We all have to settle down someday. Clearly, this is my time."

At this remark, Tweeddale set his brandy snifter atop the table with an audible thud. He laughed uneasily. "It won't happen to me, rest assured of that!"

"Whatever you say." Ramsey directed an affectionate grin at his special friend. "By the by, how is your sister today?"

He shrugged. "Fine, I suppose. Haven't seen her since the Carlisle rout."

"The songbird at Vauxhall been keeping you away from the town house?" was Durham's avid question.

"Yes," was the reluctant acknowledgment.

"Expensive piece of fluff and perfume, Ned. She'll have the duns knocking at your door, if you don't watch out," warned Ramsey.

Lord Tweeddale made some quick mental calculations. If he could only hold out until his sister was married then he would not be quite so purse pinched. Keeping the Exquisite was a strain on his finances, but well worth it. Blithely, he commented, "Beauty doesn't come cheaply. Surely, you know that."

"Gentleman's got a point. I seem to recall a French morsel you were attached to for a time, Ramsey. Angelique, wasn't it? Didn't the stunning Angelique manage to acquire a house in St. John's Wood and a sapphire necklace before it was over between you?"

The earl groaned. "Don't remind me. But I learned my lesson, and from here on, I plan to walk the straight and narrow."

"Ten pounds says you don't," Tweeddale was quick to wager.

"Make it thirty, and you've a bet," Ramsey shot back.

"Mighty sure of yourself, ain't you?" remarked Durham.

"Have you ever known me to quit midstream or back down on a promise?"

The viscount shook his head.

" 'Course not, 'cause I haven't. Thus when I pledge to be the soul of propriety, verily, I shall. Commencing with my visit to Lady Christina's establishment tomorrow afternoon." He punctuated this statement by tossing down his cards.

The game was over. As usual, Ramsey had won.

★

Park Village East, built on the fringe of Regent's Park north of Marylebone Road, was one of the many projects John Nash, the prince's architect, had conceived to enhance the city's splendor. When every design had been executed and the renovations completed, Nash promised the prince that his capital would transcend the glory of Paris. And although construction in the park was not yet finished, some twelve families had been residing in Park Village East for almost a year.

It was a noble piece of town planning. Clean and tidy, and the picture of orderly existence. The normal hubbub of the city did not trespass into this neighborhood. There were no outsiders. No beggars or vagrants, paupers or ragboys. Not even a stray dog. There was no noise save the gentle roll of carriage wheels going down the wide, tree-lined streets. Each dwelling sat back from the sidewalk in a parklike setting. Lawns were manicured, and in the warmer months, carefully pruned shrubberies and flowers abounded. The residents of Park Village East enjoyed the benefits of healthy air and the open spaces of country living as well as proximity to the conveniences of the Metropolis. It was the best of both worlds.

Life in Park Village East was the culmination of years of hard work for the merchants and senior clerks who could afford the newly constructed villas. They had left their former lives behind, yet far from aspiring to the high-flying ways of the aristocracy, they were proud to be called middle class and proud of the principles that had enabled them to quit the crowded streets of Stepney, Chick Lane, and Limehouse. Adherence to strict ethics and hard work had rewarded them abundantly, and they intended that their neighborhood prevail as a model of middle-class propriety.

Nothing was out of place in this well-ordered scheme; nothing except the large estate near the canal. It had sat in the copse of giant oaks for more than two hundred years, and unlike Nash's villas that were uniform in size and shape, Cockleshell Manse was a rambling, half-timbered Elizabethan structure. The surrounding lawns were dotted with fruit trees, an overgrown hedgerow edged the property, and a family of sheep had free range of the grounds, kept within the bounds of the Manse by an ornate wrought-iron gate at the end of a winding pebbled drive.

Hence it transpired on a Wednesday afternoon in March that The Park Village East Council of Concerned Property Owners was meeting at the home of the wool merchant,

Mr. Silas Barnaby, to settle an issue of mounting significance: what could be done to impress upon the owner of this appalling anachronism the merits of the Council's Code of Neighborhood Conduct?

The entire membership of the Council was in attendance. Some twenty-six persons were ushered into the Barnaby morning room that was, in truth, a rather small chamber for so large a gathering. At breakfast Mr. Barnaby had petitioned his wife to conduct the meeting in the formal salon, but Constance Barnaby would have none of that. She wished to show off the room that had been recently decorated in a sphinx motif, and as the will of Mrs. Barnaby generally prevailed, their neighbors were crowded into the Egyptian–style morning room. Women were perched on a variety of sofas and chairs, the legs of each piece of furniture having been molded into the bronze likeness of a sphinx. A wallpaper border, depicting the catlike creatures and alternating with pyramids, circled the room. On either side of the chimney large sphinx heads stood sentry on marble pilasters. It was an impressive sight, to be sure, and Mrs. Barnaby was well pleased by the oohs and aahs of her neighbors. It would be many months before anyone else, particularly her rival, Agatha Chudleigh, could claim ownership of so splendid and costly a morning room, she thought smugly.

Scones and tea were served by an African houseboy and the meeting officially commenced. The first order of business, after the recording secretary read the minutes of the previous meeting, was a report from Mr. Horace Cadwallader on the subject of his visit to Lady Christina Braughton of Cockleshell Manse.

Horace Cadwallader was a sinewy man, approaching middle age, who wore spectacles on the end of an extraordinarily long, questing nose. Having begun life as a stevedore on the Isle of Dogs, he had successfully climbed up the ladder of enterprise; currently, he held the deeds to more than 25 percent of the warehouses on the Thames. Tall and appearing far older than his thirty-four years, Mr. Cadwallader had the unfortunate habit of pursing his lips as if he had licked a lemon.

Puffing up with self-importance, he intoned, "As charged by this venerable Council, I presented myself at Cockleshell Manse, Friday last, but was denied access to Lady Christina."

"Well, I never," exclaimed Mrs. Chudleigh, the mill owner's wife, in a voice so shrill that the lady in question could easily have heard it from the library at Cockleshell Manse.

Mr. Barnaby shook his head in disapproval. Having been born within the sound of Bow Bells, cockney peppered his speech, particularly when he was as angry as he was at that moment. "Proves it, this does. Loike Oi was sayin', she's stuck up as those folks livin' in Mayfair. Not good enough fer the loikes of us. Just told 'er butler, no thank yer, did she? Didn't even have the decency to give yer the time of day."

"It wasn't quite like that," Mr. Cadwallader ventured to explain. "One of the beasts had taken ill, and she was tending the poor thing."

"Beasts?" squealed the covey of women. Reticules snapped open, and the sharp scent of recuperative salts pierced the air.

"Aye, beasts. Some of them from as far away as India," Mr. Cadwallader informed them.

Mrs. Chudleigh swooned.

"That does it," Silas Barnaby declared. His podgy face reddened considerably. "If a house full of beggars weren't bad enough, we come to find out she's got wild animals, too. Oi think the Council must concur Lady Christina's household is unquestionably a menace to the neighborhood."

The assembled good people of Park Village East hastily agreed, and Silas Barnaby produced a sheath of paper. He coughed several times and proceeded to read in the stentorian tones he had acquired from the merciless drills of a hired elocution tutor:

"Whereas the Lady Christina Braughton of Cockleshell Manse, Park Village East, London, has living beneath her roof no less than seven children;

"Whereas these children are not related kin to the lady;

"Whereas no male person of responsible years resides within Cockleshell Manse to guarantee the law-abiding conduct of said orphans;

"Whereas aforesaid orphans have been observed running freely through the park, unattended by any adult of competence;

"Whereas Lady Christina has failed to respond to the overtures of The Park Village East Council of Concerned Property Owners;

"Whereas aforesaid Council knows, as do all reasonable persons of common sense, that the best environment for aforesaid orphans is the Municipal Workhouse;

"And whereas the Standing Rules of The Park Village East Council of Concerned Property Owners require that residents conform to a specified code of conduct;

"And whereas Lady Christina and her household have repeatedly violated that code;

"Be it resolved that The Park Village East Council of Concerned Property Owners endeavor to remove aforesaid orphans from Cockleshell Manse."

Following a motion introduced by Mr. Chudleigh, the Council unanimously voted to commence legal proceedings against Lady Christina that afternoon.

Sunlight streamed through the mullioned windows that extended the full length of the third-floor schoolroom at Cockleshell Manse. This sun-bright and cheerful room was not the usual setting for lessons. The walls were lemon yellow; bright curtains of paisley chintz hung at the windows; twin fires blazed under carved walnut mantelpieces at opposite ends of the room; and scores of diamond-shaped panes reflected merrily on the carpeted floor.

Four children, three boys and a girl, sat behind their desks. A young woman stood in front of them. She presented a delightfully pretty picture, bathed in the warmth of the early afternoon sunshine. Thick lustrous hair, the color of aged sherry, flowed freely down her back, and the amethyst lace trim of her day dress matched the rich color of her enormous round eyes. A smile suffused her heart-shaped face as one of the boys read aloud.

23

"And so it is that the people of Somerset believe the Glastonbury Tor is hollow. There within the hollow hill, beneath the rock and earth sleeps Arthur." The handsome boy with rosy cheeks looked up from the book to glance at the woman. His expression was alive with expectancy, and when she spoke his mouth curved upward into a broad grin.

"That was very good, Finny. Thank you. Please pass the book to Lettie and she shall finish the passage for us." The woman's melodious voice flowed softly, like the sweet, merry tune of a babbling mountain brook.

"Yes, Tina mum," replied Finny. He passed the book to the freckled girl seated beside him.

Slowly, Lettie began to read, "Arthur sleeps. The King who is not dead. The King who shall one day awaken. The King who shall rise to save his people. Long live King Arthur."

"Excellent, Lettie." Tina observed the four upturned faces anxiously awaiting her next word. She smiled. "The answer to your unspoken question is, yes. We are done for the day."

The two lads nearest to one another in size, Finny and Francis, jumped to their feet.

"Hooray!"

"Can we go outside, Tina mum?"

"Of course."

"Come on, Lettie. Let's get our hoops."

In the next instant they dashed out of the schoolroom. The fourth child, a boy of ten, lingered behind.

"Joshua?" Tina addressed the eldest of her brood.

"It's Molly," the boy began. "She was crying something awful when we came back from the park yesterday."

"Why didn't you tell me earlier?" There was genuine distress in Tina's question. It was unthinkable that any of the children might have been hurt. "I must go to her straightaway."

"Oh, it isn't nothing serious, Tina mum," Joshua hastily put in.

"What then?" She paused in her flight toward the nursery door.

"It's only that she'd like to come out with us instead of staying in the nursery with Mary Katherine and Baby."

A momentary sadness crossed Tina's delicate features. Her great amethyst eyes clouded and then brightened. "How selfish I've been. Of course, Molly may join us. Today and every day. Will you bring her, please? And make certain she dresses warmly."

Tina smiled as the lad dashed off to fetch Molly. Joshua was like a father to the younger ones, looking after them and fussing over

25

them, sometimes even more than she did. He was a generous, loving boy and pride swelled within her heart, but it also ached with sorrow, for she knew the dark reasons why he was so protective. The children had been exposed to extraordinary harshness before coming to Cockleshell Manse, and in his innocence, Joshua had decided to right the evils of a world that would subject children to cruelty of any kind.

After collecting the books and replacing them on the shelf at the rear of the room, Tina took a moment to check on Francis's guinea pigs. They lived in the wooden box on the window ledge beside Finny's box turtle. The furry creatures squeaked when they saw her, and she made a mental note to ask Cook for a carrot for them.

She walked down the staircase toward her private chambers on the floor below, continuing to think about Joshua whose maturity and generosity were an endless source of amazement. Of all his deeds, the most astounding had occurred the summer when he was eight years old. Cook had sent Joshua on an errand, and the boy had returned with Francis in tow, having spent the bacon money to buy the lad from a farmer. It was abhorrent that children could still be bought and sold in this day and age, and Tina knew that she would have reacted no differently than Joshua. But she was an adult. Joshua was only a child. And that simple fact brought tears to her eyes. She was elated that the five-year-old pickpocket she had rescued from the constable had become so kind and bright a young man, and although loath to part with him, she would shortly send him to the finest public school. Joshua was destined for greatness, and Tina intended that he have every benefit to reach his full potential.

Ten minutes later, Tina descended the massive maple staircase to the great hall. It was a stately chamber, the walls wainscoted in dark wood and the ceiling beamed with timbers. Five of the children were engaged in a serious game of tag. Their giggles and shrieks of gaiety bounced off the high polished parquet floors to echo through the cavernous room.

"Are we ready?" Tina called out cheerfully. She paused on the bottom step to pull on her gloves.

The children crowded about their beloved guardian. "Yes, Tina mum," came the lively chorus of responses.

Yapping excitedly, three spaniels burst into the hall. Prince Charlie, Macbeth, and Robert Bruce — so named by Finny who had a fascination for Scottish history — circled the children, going to each one in turn to deliver a sloppy, wet lick of greeting.

"Come on, fellows!" cried Finny. "Race you to the old oak."

A whirl of dogs and boys pitched toward the front door.

"Where ye are, ye'll be stopping!" commanded a female voice in the broad flat accent of the West Country. All faces turned to watch an octogenarian couple hobble into the great hall. "Not another step without yer cloaks." It was a white-haired woman, an apron tied about her generous waist, who made the pronouncement. She turned to the stooped man who had entered at her side and instructed, "Get their cloaks, Hobbins. The mantuamaker delivered new ones yesterday. Bring those."

"Yes," came Hobbins's meek response as if he were one of the children and not the steward of the Braughton holdings for more than sixty years.

"Cook, you know better than that," Tina scolded ever so gently. "Hobbins shouldn't be lugging about our cloaks. It isn't good for his back. The boys can do it."

On a shrug Cook grumbled, "And coddling the old curmudgeon is what ye're doing, I say."

Tina ignored the remark. Cook was as irascible as Hobbins was retiring. The couple had been since her earliest memories, and they had been at odds even then. They would never change, and there was no sense in trying.

"Mild enough may the weather seem, but 'tisn't a real thaw," Cook lectured, her r's rolling out like the waves that endlessly brushed the Devonshire coast. "Not a single cuckoo will be flying out of his winter resting spot in March. And ye'll wear yer cloaks 'til he does. 'Tis weather that tricks a body and brings the ague. The young ones catching their deaths, we're not wanting, are we?"

Tina smiled at the only mother she had ever known, for her own mother had died when she was less than two. "Of course not."

Over the barking of the dogs, Francis was heard to remark, "No one better come down with a chill 'cause I don't want Cook doing any more of that hocus-pocus stuff. If I have to drink another concoction, I'll puke!"

A ripple of giggles floated through the hall. Lettie covered her mouth, little Molly followed suit, and Tina, who was hard-pressed not to laugh herself, for she well-remembered the hundreds of malodorous infusions Cook had brewed for her as a child, focused a quelling stare on the boys.

"Sorry, Tina mum," Francis mumbled

while Joshua and Finny hurried to collect the latest delivery from the mantuamaker.

Clothes were Tina's weakness. She maintained a subscription to *La Belle Assemblée,* and although she did not go about in Society and had no use for ball gowns and the like, she indulged herself by dressing the children extravagantly. The latest additions to their wardrobes were of a lighter wool than they had worn during January and February. Each boy had a burgundy military–style overcoat of fine kerseymere with smart gold-fringed epaulets at the shoulders. On their heads they wore matching burgundy visored caps. The girls had sapphire blue cloaks; the hoods were lined with auburn fox pelts. Tina, too, had a new pelisse. Hers was of a design similar to the girl's, made of the same blue merino and having a fur-lined hood added for warmth.

"Much better," said Cook as they bundled up for their walk in the park.

"Good-bye, Cook." Tina dropped a kiss on the old woman's deeply lined cheek. "We'll be back in an hour. And, I vow, not one of us plans to catch a chill."

"Harrumph!" Cook crossed her arms and glared at Tina. "Take care of wee one," she said, referring to Molly.

"Of course, Cook dear." Tina leaned down and looped the blue satin hood ribbons beneath Molly's chin. She straightened up to tie her own as the children and dogs proceeded through the heavy double door and down the front steps.

"Look at that, Cook," remarked the old man. "Master Joshua's near as tall as Lady Tina. I believe the lad may top her by summer's end."

Cook agreed, a lump rising in her throat as she moved to a window. Hobbins stood beside her, and together they watched the procession of children and dogs move across the lawn toward the stables.

"She's happy, I do believe," said Hobbins pensively. "But I can't help wishing they were her own. Wouldn't it be nice if Lady Tina could find a fine gentleman like the marquess always wanted for her?"

Cook nodded and using the edge of her apron, she dabbed at the corner of her right eye, then the left. "On that one I can't be quibbling with ye, old man."

Two

It was a splendid afternoon for an excursion to the park. The sky was clear; the air crisp with the earthy scent of an early thaw. The three boys ran ahead, Molly tagging at their heels, while Lettie walked beside Tina.

"What did Cook mean about cuckoos, Tina mum?"

"Cook's a West Country woman. She lived on a farm in Devon before she came to work for my grandfather at Ambleside, and country folk believe the cuckoo doesn't return to Britain before April. Until it does, springtime won't come."

"Oh," Lettie reflected quietly. They walked in silence for a few yards before she added, "Francis says Cook's a witch. Is she?"

Tina paused to take the girl's hand in hers. "Oh no, Lettie, you mustn't think that. Country folk simply have different ways from townspeople." It was the answer Tina had received when she had asked her grandfather that same question many years before. Like

Lettie and Francis, Tina had harbored secret fears whenever the superstitious country-woman talked about age-old customs or prepared medicinal infusions of herbs and wild plants. She added the same words with which her grandfather had concluded, "Cook loves you very much, Lettie. She isn't a witch, and she'd never do anything to hurt you."

Reassured, Lettie dashed ahead to catch up with the others.

The first stop was the carriage house to check on Gold Tabby's litter of kittens. While the girls played with the mewling balls of fluff, the boys gave an apple to Marigold, the pony.

"Can we ride the hobby horse, Tina mum?" asked Finny. They had received the pedestrian cycle on Twelfth Night.

Tina gave an affirmative response, and the lad ran off to fetch it from the storage shed. A few moments later he returned, pushing the two-wheeled vehicle by its handlebars. Tina and the children walked into the stable yard to watch Finny jump onto the seat and propel himself about the yard by pushing his feet along the ground. Every so often he achieved sufficient momentum to raise his legs in the air and cruise for several yards.

With Finny in the lead, they headed in the direction of the open park. Outside the gates of Cockleshell Manse, he picked up speed, and everyone began to run in pursuit down the tree-lined avenue. They did not stop until they reached the smooth hill in Regent's Park that ran north and south toward Marylebone Road. There the boys took turns gliding down the hill on the hobby horse.

"Don't you want a go at it, Lettie?" asked Joshua.

Timidly, she looked away. The only word she uttered was, "Can't." But the undisguised longing in her eyes belied the negative statement.

"I'll hold you up," suggested Joshua. "And I promise not to let go."

Vehemently, Lettie shook her head.

Tina crouched down until she was eye to eye with Lettie. "Would you try, if I went first?"

"Maybe."

"Splendid!" exclaimed Joshua.

Gingerly, Tina positioned herself on the hobby horse and gave a gentle push with her right boot and then her left. She had ridden it only once before and then, only for a few moments on the flat surface of the stable yard. Here on the hill in the park, one did not have to push quite as much. It was easier to pick up speed and as the wind brushed her ears, she laughed. The light, tinkling sound echoed through the bare trees as she went faster and faster. The hobby horse coursed into a slight dip, then up again, and she swallowed a gleeful laugh of surprise. Her grip on the handlebars tightened, and she dared to straighten her legs out, balancing gracefully as the wheeled vehicle soared down the hill.

"Turn, turn the handlebars," Joshua hollered through cupped hands, but Tina could not hear over the yapping of the spaniels.

Too late, she saw the gentleman directly in her path. Apparently, he had only just seen her, for his mouth was opened wide with astonishment. She was barely five or six feet away when he raised an elegant gold-tipped cane as if to protect himself from the inevitable disaster. In the next instant, Tina was jolted by the violent impact of the hobby horse slamming into the man and tossing her through the air. She felt the wind knocked from her lungs and then the peculiarly timeless sensation of soaring through space. Not daring to see where she might land, she squeezed her eyes closed and waited to hit the ground, which she did with a hollow, painful thud, the breath being punched from her once more.

"Good God, child!"

Tina heard the gentleman exclaim. She opened her eyes to see him lying prostrate on

35

the ground beside her. Her vision being somewhat fuzzy, she blinked twice before looking
again. Sweet heaven, it was Captain Ramsey,
the very gentleman she had spent the better
part of the last five years endeavoring to forget. He was stylishly dressed in a bottle green
overcoat and buckskin trousers. His beaver
hat sat atop a nearby hedge; the cane that had
proved of no defensive value whatsoever was
nowhere to be seen; Prince Charlie and
Robert Bruce were romping on his chest.
Tiny paw prints speckled his vest.

Duncan Ramsey rolled his head toward
Tina. He searched her pale face and inquired
concernedly, "Are you all right, my child?"
Then he brushed the dogs out of his way and
stood up, wincing as he put weight onto his
left leg. The full six feet plus of his lean masculine frame loomed over Tina. He held out
his hand to help her rise, but she simply lay
there staring up at him. "What is it?" he
demanded in alarm. "Can't you move? Speak
up, girl! Are you hurt?" He reached down to
assist her, but she jerked away.

A singularly cool edge tinted her words.
"I'm quite fine, sir. Merely winded and
slightly bruised. No doubt I shall suffer for
my folly on the morrow."

Joshua and the children converged on the
scene, and Tina held the older boy's arm as

she stood. "I trust you, too, are unharmed?" she addressed the gentleman who was staring at her in the most disconcerting fashion.

"Yes," Ramsey said, his voice echoing the confusion in his eyes. This girl with the heart-shaped face was not a girl at all. She was an immensely desirable young woman whose sharp words were at odds with her gentle beauty. It was no wonder he had thought her barely out of the schoolroom, for she was petite, not above five feet at best, and slender as a lily. The hood of her cape had fallen back to reveal luxuriant tawny curls and a creamy, swanlike neck that begged to be caressed. But it was her deep violet eyes that most intrigued him. Set amid flawless features, they were the most enormously round eyes he had ever beheld; eyes that reflected an innocence that was at once appealing and haunting.

"Please accept my apologies, sir," said Tina, brushing dried leaves off her pelisse, her eyes never rising to meet his curious gaze. "I am a novice rider. I thank you for your concern and trust that you shall suffer no ill from our encounter." Briskly, she faced the children. "Call the dogs, Finny. I believe it's time to start for home." On that abrupt note she led the children back up the hill.

At that precise moment Tina wanted nothing so much as to return to the Manse and retreat to the privacy of her bedchamber. She did not want to accompany the children as they gaily chanted Cock Robin, nor did she want to answer Molly's persistent questions about the handsome gentleman with the gold-tipped cane. She did not want to turn and look at the man. Most of all she did not want to remember.

But self-control is often a perverse thing, and there was no thwarting her impulse to pause halfway up the hill and glance over her shoulder. Suddenly, it seemed the world became exceedingly quiet. The singsong of the children's voices floated far away as unwanted memories came rushing back. Memories of the bittersweet summer five years before when she had been seventeen; the summer when Grandfather, the Marquess of Camden, had still been alive, and he had brought her to London for the Season. The summer when Joshua had come to live with them. The summer when she had fallen in love with Duncan Ramsey.

It was early on a sunny June morning in the year 1812, when the young Lady Christina Braughton and the Marquess of Camden left Ambleside in a state of euphoria. Ever since coming to live with Grandfather at the age of two, Tina had spent the summers alone in

Devon while the marquess was in Town. During those lonely months, she missed him dreadfully, for he was her fondest companion. He had taught her to ride and fish and hunt; he had tutored her in history, French, and Latin. And when he was gone to Town, there was no one with whom to play chess or debate the merits of mill reform and the latest child labor laws.

With typical adolescent impatience, she had passed the previous years believing this day would never come. It had seemed an eternity. Yet, finally, she was out of the schoolroom. Finally, she was not being left behind. In the throes of excitement, Tina could scarcely wait to arrive in the Metropolis. Near to exploding with anticipation, she bounced up and down on the velvet carriage squabs. Grandfather was planning a splendid comeout in her honor, and she could not get to Town fast enough.

The marquess's pleasure was similarly founded. The dearest wish of his life was about to be realized. He was going to see his darling Tina launched into Society, and as the stately black traveling coach rumbled along the London road, he breathed a sigh of relief. He had been ill that winter and had begun to fear that he might not live to see his granddaughter settled, but on this sunny spring day his fears were behind him. He and Tina were on the road to London, and she would be a veritable Diamond of the First Stare; for who would not adore his sweet Tina, his bright, bubbling, and warmhearted girl?

Upon their arrival in London there were innumerable excursions to the Burlington Arcade where Grandfather outfitted Tina as grandly as a duchess. In Miss Gower's millinery shop, she experienced her first taste of haute couture, deciding then and there that although she had spent the previous seventeen years in navy blue seersucker and white leggings, she was never going to do so again. The blossoming woman in Tina responded to the bolts of sumptuous fabrics, the dazzling rainbow of colors, and the endless parade of fashion plates from which to choose. She was infinitely fond of lilac silk and the bright yellow and green muslins that made her feel as if she were cloaked in springtime. The sparkling beaded reticules, dainty satin slippers, and lacy unmentionables were the ultimate of splendor. Grandfather thoroughly indulged her every whim; even when she admired an outrageously daring, Hyde Park bonnet of white satin with four white ostrich plumes, he purchased it, surprising her later with a pair of white kid boots to wear with it.

But clothes were not all that transformed a

schoolgirl into a Diamond of the First Stare. There were long hours spent in her dressing room with a French coiffeur in attendance. Her hair was cut and crimped and combed and pulled into a variety of styles, then color-washed, cut some more, and pinned into another battery of modish arrangements. Her nails were manicured, her skin treated with exotic, floral-scented creams, and her cheeks were faintly tinted a delicate shade of rose. Tina adored every moment of this attention. Being pampered made her feel very grown up. Little did she suspect what an insurmountable task she had presented to the purveyors of feminine beauty.

At seventeen, Tina was positively scrawny. She looked more like a boy than a girl on the threshold of womanhood. Her complexion was thoroughly colorless; her eyes were so big she resembled an insect; and the unruly curls that sprang out of her scalp were as coarse as straw.

In the end, the modiste designed a number of gowns with false bodices to hide Tina's immature figure. The Frenchman cut her hair shorter and fluffing the curls about her face like a halo, he pronounced Tina was ready to step out on her grandfather's arm.

Over the next weeks, Tina and the marquess attended an endless series of routs and balls. Through it all she smiled and answered politely when spoken to, but she did not truly pay heed to anything or anyone save the handsome Scotsman in the captain's uniform.

Duncan Ramsey, the dashing black-haired rakehell, was recently returned from a year of junior diplomatic service in Bermuda. The War of 1812 had been declared only a week before, and the ship on which he had returned to England had been engaged in a skirmish with American privateers. His tales of the battle at sea made Duncan Ramsey the recipient of much female attention, and night after night Tina watched the young captain in his bright scarlet uniform. He was forever in the company of two other rakish gentlemen, neither of whom in Tina's estimation held a candle to Captain Ramsey. He was sophisticated and virile. He had a boyishly lopsided smile, and when he laughed silver highlights twinkled in his cobalt eyes. One evening she ventured close enough to catch his voice, and the full timbre of his Highland brogue had sent little chills down her back. He was everything that was noble and gallant and brave. Soon, the gossips predicted, Captain Ramsey would go off to the Peninsula to fight with Wellington, and the thought of that handsome gentleman, so gay and untroubled at that moment, destined to die on a foreign field of battle was positively the saddest and most romantic notion Tina had ever entertained.

June turned to July, and the patronesses at Almack's sent a voucher around to the marquess in Tina's name. That same afternoon Grandfather's health began to fail. In a matter of hours he was frailer than he had been before their journey. His breathing became shallow and irregular. Tina had no intention of going to Almack's when Grandfather was ill, and they argued. The marquess would have none of her stubbornness, he stated, alleging that she would cause him to suffer a seizure of apoplexy unless she went as they had planned. Tina complied, although not enthusiastically, and the marquess arranged for Tina to go with his long-standing friends Robert Byng, the Earl of Hampshire, and his countess.

Almack's was not the dazzling success the marquess had envisioned for his granddaughter. Apprehension etched the girl's forehead. Her eyes were wide with alarm. With her mind focused on the goings-on at Grandfather's bedside, she was drab and spiritless in comparison to the other debutantes who fluttered about the assembly rooms like a flock of splendid canaries. No one — that is no one under the age of thirty — asked Tina to dance, except the Earl of Hampshire's godson.

After midnight, she actually found herself in the modifying position of sitting alone in a small alcove. Self-consciously, she opened the Belgian lace fan that had belonged to her mother and holding it beneath her eyes, unaware how protective it looked, she peered unhappily about the room. Her glance passed over the clusters of cheerful young people busily intent on the rituals of courtship, and on a second sweep across the dance floor, she saw the Earl of Hampshire. He was walking toward her, and to her amazement, Captain Ramsey was at his side.

"Young captain's asked for an introduction, Tina," the earl announced and did the necessary. Tina's eyes became even rounder. Her throat turned dry, and she swallowed hard when Duncan Ramsey executed a low bow and asked her if she would stand up with him for the next dance. A smile of such wonderment crossed her face, lighting her eyes with lavender hues, that for an instant she was positively radiant.

The captain took her arm to lead her onto the floor, and Tina flushed an unbecoming shade of crimson. "I've been watching you all evening," he whispered in an intimate aside as they formed a set with three other couples.

At this, Tina's heart skipped a beat. She stole a glimpse at Duncan Ramsey. Knowing not the first thing about flirtation, she did not dissemble, and guilelessly, she replied, "Thank you, sir. I, too, have been watching you."

The orchestra began to play, and a dark scowl marred the captain's brow as they performed the first steps of a gavotte. Tina frowned, wondering what she had done to displease him. The lively dance step separated them, and carefully, she studied her dashing partner for any hint of what was amiss, but he did not look in her direction. Then the tempo quickened. She loved to dance and the quicker the pace, the better. Her tiny feet flew above the dance floor as she gracefully executed the turns. This was the first true moment of pleasure she had experienced all evening, and Tina could not repress a giggle of delight. Her sweet, unaffected laughter rose above the music, and in that instant, Duncan Ramsey faced her. Their eyes met and she smiled shyly, but to her dismay he did not appear to share her enjoyment. Indeed, the most horrid glower shadowed his countenance for the remainder of the dance.

"Allow me to escort you to the refreshment room, Lady Tina," he said when the music ended. Happily, she accepted and slipped her arm through his as they left the ballroom. Then it happened. Without the slightest hesitation, he swung open the door to one of the cloakrooms and smoothly propelled both of them inside.

"Captain Ramsey?" she inquired, a trembling in her limbs. She knew the impropriety of being alone with any man, but the trembling was caused by something else. Anticipation. She had overheard the other girls chattering about romantic trysts on deserted balconies and in moonlit gardens. And, to the best of her limited knowledge, all of the elements necessary for seduction were present in that cloakroom. She and Duncan Ramsey were utterly alone in a small and dimly lit spot. They were away from the prying eyes of chaperons. Anything could happen, and Tina wondered if the captain intended to court her. There was an unnerving pang deep in her stomach. Her voice quivered when she repeated his name, "Captain Ramsey?"

"Yes?" He responded with a question, the single low word wrapping about her like a sheet of smooth, sun-warmed satin.

"What do you want, Captain?" Tina's breathless question was barely above a whisper.

"Can't you guess?" He moved closer and slipped an arm around her waist.

In that second the vital male warmth of him transmitted to Tina. Her blood was racing frantically, and when he ran the back of his hand across her cheek Tina feared her heart might burst. She knew then that he was going to kiss her, and she neither hesitated nor wondered why. It was up to her to naysay him, but she did not pull away. Gladly, she received the lips of this man who would soon sail across the Channel to meet his fate.

The kiss was feather-light. His lips barely touching hers while his strong hands cupped her shoulders to hold her steady. A small sigh of wonder escaped her lips. She closed her eyes and inhaled the scent of him; her mouth opened slightly to taste the brandy on his lips. Her body was tingling all over, and instinctively, she wound her hands about his forearms and swayed against his hard chest. Sensations she had never dreamed of pulsed through her. For an instant, she thought she was on the beach below the cliffs at Ambleside, the Atlantic surf tugging at her, washing over her.

Of a sudden, she heard the captain groan. A harsh sound was torn from his throat as if he were in pain, and his grip tightened, roughly pulling her against the length of him. His lips moved down the curve of her neck, his breath caressing her skin. Then he wrenched himself free.

Tina stared in wonder and perplexity as he

47

framed her face with his hands. An eternal moment of silence stretched between them. One of his fingers pushed a stray curl off her temple. His eyes searched hers.

"I should never have done that, Lady Tina," he said in a low and serious tone of voice.

Instantly, she knew what he was going to say next.

"Please, don't apologize," she said quickly. "That would quite ruin the most extraordinarily special moment of my life, Captain." In response he said nothing, and shyly, she continued, "You see, I've never been kissed before, and I had quite feared that it might be unpleasant, but that was not the case at all."

Duncan Ramsey appeared to whiten before her eyes. "Be that as it may, Lady Christina" — his voice was harder now — "it was highly improper of me, and you should not let any more gentlemen kiss you in cloakrooms!"

She did not know what to make of his words. They were distinct enough, but it was certainly not the way she had imagined a romantic interlude would unfold. Seconds later the matter was clarified. From the other side of the paper-thin wall came two males' voices.

"By damn! Ramsey did it. Never thought he'd have the stomach to actually kiss such an

48

ugly squab, did you?"

" 'Course, I did. Ramsey's a sportsman, and when the wager's high enough he'll do anything."

They laughed heartily. Tina's stomach plummeted to the floor, and as their voices faded away she raised an unsteady hand to her cheek. It was hot with shame. There was no denying what they were discussing, nor the truth of her encounter with Duncan Ramsey. Verily, he did not possess a shred of interest in her; he had merely been flirting. No, she corrected, he had seduced her to win a bet.

She tried to speak and failed.

"My apologies," he said stiffly. Then he turned on his heel and left.

That was the last Tina saw of Captain Ramsey, and she mollified her pain with the consolation that she would likely never set eyes on him again, for a man so cruel deserved to be skewered on a French bayonet.

A fortnight later the marquess's physician informed Tina that there was little hope for improvement in Grandfather's condition. The winter fever had taken an irreparable toll. Grandfather would not recover his former health, but his days could be prolonged if they left the city for healthier climes. So Tina returned to Ambleside, quite heartbroken, her dreams having been dashed, and the future looking decidedly bleak.

In the first week of September, the marquess succumbed to the lung inflammation. Through Grandfather's death, she experienced the true pain of loss, thereby making the discovery that she had never really loved the captain. She had merely fancied herself in love with all that she thought he represented. It was not her heart that had been hurt, rather her pride was wounded. Having learned this valuable lesson she was able to assess the Society of which her grandfather had wanted her to be a part. At the age of seventeen, Tina decided that if she had the choice, she would elect to live her own life, not to be a wife, nor ever again be subject to the whim of any man.

When the marquess's will was read, Tina was given that opportunity. She found herself in possession of one of the greatest fortunes in the realm. A generous allowance and the lands in Devonshire and London were hers, the sole condition being the appointment of an aged Scots earl as guardian. As fate would have it, the earl was quite as eccentric as Grandfather; he never sought to dictate to Tina, and from the outset she was left to her own devices.

Grandfather had left her the most precious legacy conceivable: independence.

She remained in Devon for another full year, and during that time Lettie and Finny joined the household. The following summer a fire razed Ambleside, and Tina conceived no option save to pack up the children and return to the rambling London house that sat on the bank of an old canal in Regent's Park. It was a move she undertook with some trepidation, for her memories of London were not pleasant ones.

This time, however, London was quite perfect. Tina's family grew. Life at Cockleshell Manse was joyous and carefree. She was content to be mistress of her own establishment, surrounded by love and in return, sharing her heart and her bounty with others. There was nothing she needed. Everything was as it should be. And nothing would ever hurt her again. Or so she had thought until colliding with Duncan Ramsey.

Well, she thought, rousing herself from the past, it was nothing more than a chance encounter. It was bound to have happened sooner or later, and it did not countenance in the least.

Oh, but it did matter, she corrected. It mattered very much.

Too well did she recall their kiss, the lilt of his full-bodied voice, the warmth of his body. And the horrible fact that Duncan Ramsey had not even recognized Tina affected her more profoundly than anything since Grandfather's death. Although the children's plight had touched her tender nature, her own emotions had been inured since that summer five years before. She had cried for Molly and Finny and Mary Katherine, but not once, in all that time, had she cried for herself. She had never denied that the captain had held her in low regard to have treated her so shabbily, but not even to remember her face was a devastating blow that Tina had been unprepared to confront. Clearly, he held no memory of her, nor of that brief summer moment they had shared. That was the saddest part of it; he did not recall the very incident that had immutably shaped her existence.

Three

" 'Twas a bang-up collision, Cook!" declared Francis as he led the way into the library where a fire crackled merrily in the two-storied hooded hearth. "The both of them went flying in the air like a pack of hounds who've caught the scent of a fox."

As the elderly woman checked Tina for broken bones, she emitted several reproachful clucks. "Told ye that French contraption was a danger."

"I'm fine," Tina assured, placing her gloves on a table.

The old woman shook her head. "A body ain't fine when it's been tossed through the air like a bag of flour!"

"But she was very brave," put in Molly on a solemn nod, and everyone's attention shifted to the details of the accident.

Lettie giggled. "You should have seen the gentleman, Cook. He was the veriest Incomparable."

"Oh, Lettie, don't be such a goose!" Francis cast a disgusted glance at the girl. "You can't call a gentleman an Incomparable. He was Top o' the Trees!"

"Well, whatever he was, he was positively splendid," she said on a sigh. "And Tina mum thought so too. Did you see the way she looked at him?"

Tina heard not a word being spoken. As the children regaled Cook with a full recounting of the incident, she walked across the library to stand before the ornate rosewood mirror suspended above an escritoire.

Was she so much changed these past five years? Tina wondered, studying the image of the slender woman who stared back at her. Having never been vain, Tina saw what she had always seen. Before her stood a young lady who did not appear her full twenty-three years. She saw a pair of large amethyst eyes set in the middle of what she considered tolerably well-balanced features. Everything was as it had always been. Granted, she had filled out about the bodice, and last year, her waist had started to nip in nicely of its own accord. The only significant change was her hair. She had not cut it over the past five years, and as it had grown out, it had softened like silk, becoming a tawnier, deeper color. That was certainly different. But for the rest of it, Tina saw the same girl who had been ill-used by

Captain Ramsey.

"Cocoa and biscuits!" announced Hobbins as he entered the room pushing a tea cart, his words pulling Tina from her meditation. Nurse brought Mary Katherine and Baby down from the nursery, and within minutes the hobby horse accident was no longer of interest to the children. They turned their attention to the black currant preserves and peppermint sticks that Hobbins had included on the tea tray. The two youngest girls settled into the window seat to play with their dolls. Francis and Finny brought out the draughts and board, and lay down on the rug before the hearth to set up the game. Lettie, who was trying ever so hard to be a young lady, sat at the pianoforte to practice her scales. Joshua picked up *Robinson Crusoe* and began to read chapter three. And Tina, holding Baby in her arms, reclined on a scrolled sofa that was set at an angle to the fireplace; she slipped off her walking shoes and wriggled her toes toward the warmth of the fire. Baby bounced up and down and gurgled as she endeavored to eat the lace trim on Tina's gown.

It was upon this model scene of domestic tranquillity that Duncan Ramsey entered the library at Cockleshell Manse.

Hobbins opened the door, stepped three paces over the dark red Herat carpet, then moved one step to the side to admit Ramsey. "Earl of Croick." His presentation was a bit rusty, having not announced a peer of the realm since the marquess's funeral.

Puzzled, Tina sat up and peered around the corner of the sofa. Her heart almost froze. There was Duncan Ramsey, standing on the threshold of her library, his smart outfit rather worse for the wear and looking as infuriatingly handsome as ever. To her horror, giggles drifted across the room from the direction of the window seat.

"It's him!" declared Lettie. "Isn't he smashing?"

"Top o' the Trees," corrected Francis.

The girls collapsed into a second peal of giggles.

"Yes?" Tina croaked out, so absorbed in her own dismay that she did not notice Duncan Ramsey's blatant bewilderment.

"I believe there must be some error. I've come to call on Lady Christina. Is she at home?" he barely got the words out.

"There is no mistake, my lord. I am Lady Christina," she announced, apprehension in her voice. What was he doing here? Had he followed her back from the park? Had he finally recalled that night at Almack's? And why had Hobbins called him the Earl of Croick?

Ramsey hardly knew what to say next. He was stunned by the presence of the young lady with whom he had collided in the park. This delightful miss was the antidote whom the tabbies claimed had not taken? Inconceivable! What was it Durham had said about her Season? Scorned by love? Impossible! Only a fool would do naught but welcome such a beauty with open arms. Not only was Lady Christina lovely to behold, but also she was in possession of an uncommon poise. Unaccountably, he felt as if he had misplaced all but a modicum of his usual charm. Self-consciously, he glanced about the room, awkwardly shifting his weight from the cane to his good leg and then back to the cane.

Tina was no less stupefied. What was she to do? She could not simply demand to know why he was there, nor could she order him to leave her home without explanation. It was at times like this, Grandfather had often counseled Tina, that good breeding and the perfection of the rules of etiquette proved invaluable. When in doubt, do the right, had been his motto. So, following Grandfather's advice, Tina took a steadying breath and politely offered, "Would you care to take tea with us, my lord?"

Thankful for the diversion and the opportunity to rest his leg, Ramsey accepted. He took the seat on the other side of the hearth.

Silence descended on the room while Tina poured. She dared not look up, fearing the derision she might discover in his regard, for if he had remembered who she was then surely he could think of her with naught but pity.

"It isn't really tea," Molly's high voice broke the silence. "It's cocoa."

"I trust cocoa is all right," said Tina on an anxious note.

"Oh, but I love cocoa. Truly. In fact, I haven't had a good cup in ages. Are those peppermint sticks?" he inquired, a touch of boyish hope coloring his words.

"Yes," said Molly, thoroughly besotted by the tall handsome gentleman. She was a chubby girl with a winning smile and long black braids, and as she inched her way closer to Ramsey's side he smiled at her. Molly dimpled engagingly in return.

"When I was a lad I used to stir my hot chocolate with peppermint sticks. Nurse allowed it only on the most special occasions. I don't suppose I'd be permitted to do that here, would I?" A lock of dark hair fell across his forehead. His eyes sparkled and over the top of Molly's head, he winked at Tina.

"Oh yes, sir. It would be fine. You're allowed," responded Molly, ever serious.

Ramsey smiled broadly, dipped the peppermint stick into the cup, and licked a drop of chocolate off the end. The children beamed their approval, and he relaxed. "Reading *Robinson Crusoe*, I see," he remarked to Joshua.

"Yes, sir. Have you read it?"

"Years ago as a schoolboy. It was splendid."

"Oh, indeed, it is, sir. A right jolly tale. I'd be pleased to lend you my copy, if you'd like to read it again, sir."

He was taken aback by this generous offer. These children did not know him. He was a stranger, and yet they were accepting him with an openness one did not often encounter. "These charming children are your brothers and sisters?" he finally looked at his hostess and managed to inquire.

A little laugh was set free from Tina's tautly held body, releasing some of her own inner tension. "No. This is my family."

"Then you are married?"

"No," she answered quietly, her gaze shifting to where her fingers tweaked at the ties on Baby's woolen booties.

Aware of the impropriety of his questions, Ramsey coughed. He stumbled over his words, "Please excuse my boldness, Lady Christina. You see, I had not expected you to be so young. What I mean to say is — " He broke off in mid-sentence to stare dumbfounded at Lady Christina. That he was handling this no better than a green lad was not the reason why he was so flabbergasted. Rather it was the expression on the lady's face. There he saw adoration mingled with anguish, and it stopped him cold, for he could not help feeling that he had met this woman before, yet he knew it was impossible.

"Yes?" she said with a touch of disappointment and relief since his words indicated he still did not recall the past. Perhaps, Tina thought on a long, drawn breath, it was better this way. "Go on," she prompted. Her eyes remained focused on Baby's feet.

"The fact is I recently inherited my uncle's title and lands, and my solicitor has informed me my uncle was obliged to monitor your estate."

Tina looked up. A frown crossed her face. Sharply, she said, "If it is your understanding that your uncle was recently my guardian, you are mistaken, my lord. I am of age and answer to no one save myself."

The frigid quality of this statement startled Ramsey. The fragile easy mood had been broken and once more he faltered. "Well, no. Don't believe anyone was ever meant to manage the funds except yourself, my lady. We're related, you know, distant cousins."

"That's impossible!" In a fiercely protective gesture, she hugged Baby tightly to her chest.

"Seems my grandmother, Cecilia Braughton, was your grandfather's sister. I believe that makes us third cousins. We've a set of great-grandparents in common."

There was no reason to doubt the truth of his words; Grandfather had often talked about his elder sister who had married a Highland laird. In response to this astounding news her mouth formed a silent "Oh." She was related to Duncan Ramsey? Her heart beat faster, and she said, "I had not known that I had any living relations."

"Nor I." His grin melded into a charming smile. "Which is really why I called. Seems your grandfather asked my uncle to keep an eye on you. He was bedridden the past four years, and I don't guess he ever did so himself, but when my solicitor informed me you were unmarried, I thought I'd check and see how you were getting along." Egad, Ramsey! he berated himself. You're bungling this. Why don't you go ahead and accuse her of being on the shelf while you're at it? Why don't you tell her what a lonely, old spinster you assumed she was? he taunted silently.

"As you can see we're quite fine," she said,

wishing this interview were at an end.

"Well, yes." Embarrassed, his eyes fled her probing amethyst ones to wander about the room, resting on each of the children who had been avidly listening. "Didn't mean to sound reproving, Lady Christina."

She heard the contrition in his voice and followed the direction of his gaze. "Would you like to meet my children?" He gave an affirmative nod, and automatically, the children lined up in order of height, beginning with Joshua. Tina's voice came lighter when she said, "This is my oldest boy, Joshua. And my eldest girl, Lettie. Next we have Finny and Francis. Nine and eight respectively. This pretty young thing is Molly, and hiding behind her is Mary Katherine."

The boys executed courtly bows. The girls curtsied elegantly.

"Baby!" whispered Molly. "Don't forget Baby."

"Ah yes. Thank you, Molly. And this is Baby. Unfortunately, we haven't agreed on her name. Molly and Mary Katherine are fond of Polka Dot, and the boys favor Candy. My personal choice is Sarah, but until we agree, she remains Baby."

Duncan Ramsey's mouth opened and closed several times. "But how? If you're unmarried, Lady Christina." He looked first at the children and then back at Tina.

To her absolute surprise she witnessed something she never thought to observe. Duncan Ramsey flushed a dull red, and in that instant, she saw him not as the crass young captain he had once been, but merely as the gentleman whom she had encountered earlier that afternoon in the park. She did not know what kind of man he was, but instinctively, she sensed that the passage of time and the adversities of war had made a different person of him. Her tone of voice was warmer when she said, "Let them tell you."

"Tina saved me from the constable when I was only five," announced Joshua. "Though I'm not proud of it, I was a pickpocket, sir. Snatched Tina mum's reticule in the Pantheon Bazaar, I did, and got nabbed for it, right and good. No telling what would have happened, if she hadn't talked her Grandfather into letting me live with them."

Lettie stood beside the pianoforte. In an exceedingly serious tone of voice, she said, "My mama was Mrs. Evangeline Whitherspoon, the leading actress with Reginald Armstrong's Thespian Entertainments, but she ran away with a sailor in Falmouth and the company lost its contract and there was no money, so they left me by the side of the road. Tina mum and Joshua were riding in the pony cart when they found me and took me home to Ambleside."

Next Finny and Francis stepped forward. Finny spoke first, "I was born in Ireland, sir, and was bound for Boston with my Mam, but she died on the ship between Dublin and Falmouth, and they put me off there. Hobbins found me on the wharf, sir, and brought me home to Tina mum."

"And I was bought, sir," Francis stated with a peculiar sort of pride.

"As in purchased?" Duncan Ramsey had never heard of such a thing.

"Yes, sir. I was indentured to a farmer who needed money for whiskey. He sold me to Joshua for two crowns."

"We're gallows babies," Molly said, pointing to herself and Mary Katherine.

Ramsey could not utter a word. He had heard about the infants born and raised within the walls of Newgate, and it turned his stomach to think of children living in such a hell-hole. After a long breath, he looked at Tina with open respect. Quietly, he asked, "And Baby?"

"Someone simply left her on our doorstep," was Tina's answer.

"Tell him when. Tell him when," chorused the children.

"Baby was a Christmas present. Weren't

you, my darling?" She planted a kiss on the babe's pink forehead. "She wasn't very old. Perhaps only two or three months, but she's grown up a great deal since December, and we're exceedingly proud of her. She has four teeth, and she's beginning to crawl. Watch." Tina set Baby on the carpet, but Ramsey, spellbound by the sight of Tina, did not watch the infant.

With fascination, he observed the wealth of love and tenderness that suffused her expression. Lady Christina was the most enchanting woman he had ever encountered. The affection reflected within the depths of her eyes enhanced an already spectacular natural beauty. She was positively ethereal. Again somewhere deep within him a memory was crying out. Lady Christina reminded him of someone he had once known, someone who had touched his mortal soul.

"I'm sure you must think it presumptuous of me to intrude on your privacy like this," he said soberly, having comprehended how ridiculous it would be to suggest that she join his household as a companion to Penelope. How wrong he had been to assume that because she lived apart from Society she must be lonely. Lady Christina's life was fuller than those of most people of his acquaintance.

"Not at all." Tina leaned down and picked

up Baby. Automatically, she adjusted the tiny lace collar of the infant's cambric dress. The humble, almost apologetic tenor in his voice made her exceedingly uncomfortable, and she added dismissively, "You were merely doing what you believed best."

Ramsey, for his part, paid undue attention to the last sip of cocoa on the bottom of the cup. Why did she make him feel like a lad in leading strings? There was no derision in her words. She had spoken softly, sincerely, yet he felt exceedingly foolish.

"I can see you're quite fine, Lady Christina," he said deferentially, then experienced the unexpected wish that she was not so self-sufficient. Damn, but the woman was near perfect! he surprised himself with such unexpected resentment. Yes, she was quite fine. Verily, the lady was more than fine, and Duncan Ramsey decided that he very much liked what he saw in her. She was no milk-and-water miss. Lady Christina was a woman of character, in possession of the most admirable blend of traits: inner fortitude and tenderness. A rare union, indeed, Ramsey believed, and one that only the finest individuals attained.

What the snobbish high-sticklers said about Park Village East did not figure into his evaluation of Lady Christina. He saw no reason to meddle with her situation. Cockleshell Manse was a perfect setting for her. It was her home, and plainly, she cared not one whit for the company of Society or its approval. It was refreshing to find a woman, or anyone for that matter, who was content with her lot in life. Christina Braughton had been blessed to find such happiness.

Oh, what a marvel it would be, he thought with unforeseen wistfulness, if he could be so fortunate in the path he pursued. Would that his future be a bright one. His own childhood had not been nearly as joyful as the one this lively flock enjoyed. They, too, had lives to be envied. That single thought led to another, and there, sitting in Lady Christina's library, he was struck by the paramount desire to never leave Cockleshell Manse.

Ramsey set the empty cup on the table. "Perhaps you might allow me to call on you and your family again. Out of respect for your grandfather and my uncle, of course," he amended, his blue eyes dancing at the prospect of paying visits to the lady and her unique household.

This was not what Tina had expected him to say. It threw her off balance, and she paused a moment, noticing the children's hopeful expressions. Unable to deny them anything, she responded unwittingly, "That would be fine. We would be pleased to receive you any-time at Cockleshell Manse."

He rose to leave, and she offered him her hand.

"Your servant, my lady," he said, raising her hand to his lips.

"My lord," she replied, exquisitely aware of the strength in those long lean fingers, excruciatingly conscious of the warmth of his lips.

On the threshold of Cockleshell Manse, Tina leaned against the stout oak-paneled door and watched him walk down the drive. For the first time she noticed that he limped. He must have been wounded on the Continent, she realized, experiencing a twinge of remorse that she had once wished he might be run through by an enemy saber. Finny and Francis accompanied him to the end of the drive. Obviously, they liked Duncan Ramsey. It was easy to see why. He was exceedingly charming. And she was obliged to acknowledge that he was as handsome as she remembered. No, actually he was better. The cocky appeal was gone, replaced by a bold maturity she did not recall. Fine lines flared out at the corners of his eyes and deepened when he smiled, which he did considerably more often than the young captain had done. There had been nothing condescending in the manner in which he had conversed with Joshua. That he possessed a sensitive gentler side was apparent in the way he returned the girls' shy smiles.

Sighing deeply, Tina wrapped her arms about her waist. She reflected that she was well past the age of falling into raptures over any gentleman, especially if that man was Duncan Ramsey. What then, she wondered, accounted for the strange stirring within her breast as she watched him wave farewell to the boys?

Four

On Friday, Tina received Horace Cadwallader and Agatha Chudleigh in the Winter Saloon at Cockleshell Manse.

"I'm dreadfully sorry," she told Mr. Cadwallader when he related the tale of his previous, unproductive visit. "Please, believe that I'm never too busy to receive callers. Hobbins should have asked you to wait 'til I finished attending to Black Jack."

"You ought to dismiss the man," Agatha Chudleigh stated in a superior tone of voice. "No room for shirkers and the like in this world. If a body can't do his job right and proper, then he ought to be shown the door. Surely, you know that, Lady Christina."

"I'm sorry you don't approve of my tolerance, Mrs. Chudleigh." Tina bit her tongue to prevent a harsher retort. The Chudleigh woman's lack of charity was most disheartening. She endeavored to explain, "Hobbins has loyally served four generations of Braughtons over more than six decades, and I consider him part of my family. Why, where would he go?"

"I'm sure it's no concern of mine," Agatha Chudleigh responded without a thread of feeling.

Horace Cadwallader on the other hand was not so compassionless. "It's an admirable thing you're doing, Lady Christina. A man cannot be productive his entire life, but he ought not to be discarded simply because he becomes too old to continue at the same pace."

"Thank you, Mr. Cadwallader," Tina replied archly.

A faint blush heightened the merchant's complexion, and Agatha Chudleigh observed the unfolding events with displeasure. How dare the man simper in this woman's presence? Lady Christina was a disgrace to her peers; why else did she reside in isolation as she did? Moreover her conduct vis-à-vis the Council's standards was of equal infamy. Any woman who dared to live alone was quite the far side of respectable. Besides, this was not a social visit. They had come for one purpose only. A purpose that, Agatha Chudleigh surmised, was in jeopardy; Horace Cadwallader was being sadly bamboozled by this hussy. She nearly choked on one of Cook's hot buns when Horace looked at Lady Christina and inquired:

"And Black Jack? How is the patient faring?"

"Oh, he's quite recovered, thank you. It was nothing more than an overgrown claw, but it makes the children feel better, if a great fuss is made of cutting them. Would you care to see him?"

"Why, yes, I'd like that very much, if you please," Horace Cadwallader answered. He stood so quickly that Agatha Chudleigh was surprised he did not overturn the entire tea tray.

They strolled down the long gallery toward the conservatory. Mrs. Chudleigh dawdled several paces behind and fumed silently about the foolishness of all men when they found themselves within forty paces of a pretty face. Her glance darted between Horace Cadwallader and Lady Christina in consternation. The Council should never have nominated an unmarried man to this task.

"Exotic birds have always fascinated me, Lady Christina," he said conversationally. "I started working on the docks when I was seven, and I'll never forget the first time a ship came in from the East. Ceylon, it was, and a marvel to see the coolies on board and smell the tea and spices. But 'twas the cockatoos what caught my fancy. Seems the Company man was bringing several home for his children."

Reaching the conservatory, they entered and wound their way through a profusion of hothouse flowers. Black Jack was perching docilely on the limb of an orange tree. "Hello, Polly!" he screeched. Somewhere on the other side of the glass-enclosed room a second bird answered. There were several ornate cast-iron chairs arranged beneath the orange trees, and Tina motioned for her guests to be seated.

"That's how we got Black Jack," commented Tina. "He's a macaw. A family friend obtained him while posted in Guiana. We've a cockatoo as well. From Malaya. Have you been abroad, Mr. Cadwallader?"

"No. Farthest I've been in a boat is Gravesend. Someday I hope to travel. It would be nice to see where all that stuff comes from," he confessed his fondest wish.

The sincerity in his tone of voice worried Mrs. Chudleigh. It was time to get back to the business at hand. None too tactfully she said, "We didn't come to chitchat, Lady Christina. Horace, please, explain the reason why we're here."

Horace Cadwallader was appalled by Mrs. Chudleigh's lack of subtlety. Lady Christina was not the scarlet woman he had expected to meet. She had welcomed them into her home most sincerely. How could he tell her what the Council intended? The words stuck in his throat. The only thing that he could manage was, "Well, you see, Lady Christina. You see, we represent the Park Village East Citizens Council. And, you see," he stuttered and finally stopped speaking altogether.

Mrs. Chudleigh took command. "What Mr. Cadwallader is failing to explain is that the Council met Wednesday past, and by unanimous vote declared its intention to petition the courts to remove the urchins from Cockleshell Manse to the local workhouse."

For a few moments Tina was robbed of the ability to speak. "By urchins are you referring to the children who live with me?" she asked, barely able to credit what she had heard.

"That is exactly what I mean," Mrs. Chudleigh said in a haughty tone.

Tina's expression grew concerned. "The Council wishes to send them to the workhouse? Why is that, Mrs. Chudleigh?"

"Tsk. Tsk," she clucked. "The reasons should be clear. This is hardly the proper environment for children. You are not married, Lady Christina. There is no man to supervise this household. Moreover, as anyone knows, hard work never hurt a soul. 'Tis good for children. Builds character."

"Do you agree with this?" Tina asked Horace Cadwallader who had the grace to look discomposed as he nodded a weak response. Hurt and anger roiled within Tina. Swiftly, she rose to her feet and faced Mrs. Chudleigh.

"Of you, madam, who have shown nothing but arrogance since entering my home, I find such a narrow-minded attitude in keeping with your nature. But from you, Mr. Cadwallader, I am surprised. My children are not urchins. They are merely young ones who need love and gentle guidance. They have already seen enough of life's harder side to give them the resolve to succeed at whatever they endeavor. They already possess a healthy respect for hard work. Mr. Cadwallader, you said that you went to work on the docks at age seven. From what Joshua and Finny have told me, I understand the docks are a brutal world. It is a tribute to what little kindness mankind bestows on his weaker brothers, sirrah, that you survived and have done so much. I am merely trying to do for these children that which you have done for yourself. I am merely trying to give them the chance for better lives than the ones into which they were born. You of all people should have more mercy."

Before Horace had the time to gather his thoughts, Mrs. Chudleigh spoke. "Be that as it may, Lady Christina, the Council has voted and engaged the services of a solicitor. A legal notice will be served within a sennight."

Tina shook with a fine fury. Her eyes flashed dangerously. "This is my home, and I have not broken any laws. Neither am I in need of a husband to run my life, nor the sanction of the Citizens Council to allow whomever I please to reside beneath my roof. I will thank you to leave Cockleshell Manse. You, most especially, Mrs. Chudleigh, are not welcome on my property."

"Well, I never!" the sharp-tongued woman harrumphed in response to this valediction, then pulled her skirts closer to swish past Tina. With her nose in the air, she barbed, "You're mighty uppity, missy. But we'll see how high-and-mighty you truly are when you're called before the magistrate!"

Horace Cadwallader, unable to meet Tina's eye, followed in his neighbor's wake.

The following morning dawned gray and bleak. The thaw had passed, and the weather turned shockingly cold. Temperatures dropped below the freezing mark, and a biting wind whipped off the Thames. It was barely ten o'clock when a hired chaise arrived at Cockleshell Manse to transport Tina to the offices of the Honorable Mr. T. D. Bentham, barrister-at-law.

There, seated before the only window in a

musty room cluttered with law books and court files, Tina told the barrister about the Park Village East Citizens Council.

"In your opinion, Mr. Bentham, have I broken the law?"

The barrister shifted uncomfortably behind his desk before replying. "Therein rests the problem, my lady." He gestured at the books about the room. "Within those pages lie a mere pittance of the hundreds, nay thousands, of laws in the statutes. Verily, any law enacted within the past six hundred years remains in force, and sadly, our legal system is burdened with feudal relics. Thus I cannot say for certain that somewhere there is not a statute you may have transgressed."

"What sort of statute, Mr. Bentham?" Tina dreaded the answer, and she folded her hands to still their trembling.

"There might be a law that requires orphans to reside under the care of a parish poor relief system or one that precludes unmarried women from being property owners. There are countless laws that have been forgotten for hundreds of years, but if your neighbors wish to make trouble, Lady Christina, I'm afraid they can. They need only locate a single obscure statute and a magistrate willing to enforce it."

Tina's hands became moist with anxiety.

She forced herself to ask, "Are you saying the courts might be able to take the children from me?"

"Yes."

Stunned by the possibility of being placed on trial like a common criminal, frightened by the prospect of having a magistrate commit the children to a workhouse, Tina ran a shaking hand across her eyes. Bitterly, she said, "That doesn't sound like a system that upholds justice, Mr. Bentham."

The gentleman agreed. "You would find little argument on that point. Legal reform is much debated these days. However, it shall be years before changes are effected, and thus you and I, my lady, must deal with the current system and its myriad imperfections."

Teasing her lower lip between her teeth, Tina thought for a moment. "Might I adopt the children? If they were legally members of my family would that not change the situation in my favor?"

"I'm afraid not. Firstly, under the Common Law the right to adopt is granted only to men. As a woman you can neither adopt a child nor legally take one into your wardship. And secondly, adoption is only recognized by the courts as the means for a man who has no sons to legally identify an heir of his own choosing. Again, that right is preserved solely for men."

"What should I do then?" she asked, experiencing the dreadful feeling that her world was about to unravel around her. The encounter with Duncan Ramsey was a shock, but this was unspeakable. What would she tell the children? Should they return to Devon? No! The one thing that she would not do was run away as if she were guilty. Whatever Mr. Bentham told her, she would remain at Cockleshell Manse.

"Regretfully, I have no advice at this time, Lady Christina. Until I have reviewed the document in question, there is little to be done. We must wait for the Council to act."

On that dispiriting note the meeting concluded. Tina promised to return once a formal charge had been served, and having thanked the barrister for his time, she exited the trim brick building so preoccupied with her thoughts that she would neither have seen nor heard a riot had she stumbled into a raging street fracas.

She saw nothing as she wandered in the vague direction of Regent's Park. Hence she did not see Duncan Ramsey entering Minton's Haberdashery in the company of Lord Tweeddale.

Had she been watching she would have seen much more than that. As the gentlemen entered the shop, a girl wearing a bishop's blue bonnet, curls peeping from beneath the brim, ducked behind a parked mail coach. Had Tina been watching it would have been patently obvious that the girl was hiding from one of the gentlemen. In truth, it was the Honorable Penelope Latham, and she was assiduously avoiding her brother and her fiancé.

Penelope breathed a sigh of relief. It would have been a loathsome scene if Ned had discovered her wandering the streets without her maid. He would likely have delivered a most tiresome set down and that was something Penelope desired to avoid almost as much as Duncan Ramsey. A full week had passed since Penelope had last seen her betrothed, and she could not have been happier.

Reassured that the gentlemen in question had gone, Penelope darted from her hiding place and hailed a hansom. On this bitter day she had only one goal in mind, and she did not intend that anyone or anything stop her from reaching Smithfield Market before noon. Ten minutes later the hired carriage halted before an empty warehouse. There was no trace of the lowing cattle and bleating flocks of sheep that, in the fairer weather, were corralled into pens stretching across several acres of bare ground known as Smithfield Market. Three brightly painted gypsy caravans were all that occupied the great open space. Bells hung from the wagons' eaves, chiming discordantly with the clang of pots and harnesses swinging alongside them.

Suddenly, the shutters on one of the wagons flung open and a gypsy poked out her head.

"You there! What do you want, girl?" she asked in a harsh and mysterious accent.

Penelope squeaked and almost ran off, but she had come this far and it would be the outside of foolishness to turn back. After a fortifying gulp of frigid air, she dared to ask:

"Are you Madame Zaborini?"

"Who asks?" The woman's olive skin was deeply lined about the mouth and eyes; her heavy brows were dark as charcoal. From beneath an exotic silk scarf that was bound about her head tumbled several hanks of ink black hair. Her lips were bright red as was the large glass amulet that hung from a cord about her neck. As she leaned forward the bead made a musical sound, hitting against the chains of copper and silver draped across her chest. She squinted at Penelope and repeated her question.

"I do," was Penelope's faint response.

"And what does *I* want with Madame

Zaborini?" the Romany woman demanded forbiddingly.

"I should like to have my fortune told, if you please."

"Aah!" Golden coins hanging from her earlobes jangled. She smiled and showed one black tooth, then motioned to the back of the wagon. "Enter."

Penelope climbed into the wagon. It was dark and smoky, bitter aromas like the incense that was burned at St. George's on Easter clung to the air, and in one corner coals burned in an iron brazier. Crates and baskets littered the floor, making it difficult to maneuver to the middle where the gypsy waited on a bench. After stepping over several bundles of clothes that suspiciously favored sleeping children, Penelope reached the bench and sat down opposite the olive-skinned woman.

Madame Zaborini took Penelope's hand and turned it over. With a dry brown finger she traced the lines in the petal-soft palm and muttered some mumbo jumbo in a guttural tongue. "No good. No good for dukering. I must do tea leaves, instead. You have money?" she inquired while she poured tea into a cracked blue and white cup.

"Yes." Penelope opened her reticule and showed her money to the woman.

Grinning, Madame Zaborini pushed the cup toward Penelope. "You drink."

Penelope took a sip. It was a nasty, acrid brew, hardly similar to any tea she had ever tasted, but she drank it obediently. When a tea leaf stuck between her teeth, she decided that she had had quite enough and set the cup down on the overturned barrel that served as a table.

The gypsy nodded. "We begin." She picked up the cup and held it beneath a lantern, turning it this way and that, studying its contents with noteworthy intensity. After several minutes of excruciating silence, she spoke. "I see your future. It comes closer through the mists. Aiya! You will be very happy." She raised one eye to measure Penelope's reaction to this revelation. The girl appeared contented so she continued, "I see countryside. Much water. And I see girl with blond hair. It is you! And beneath a tree, I see a man. Aiya! He is handsome man."

"Yes?" The breath caught in Penelope's throat.

"I see tall man. Nobleman, perhaps, a duke. Now, I see clearly. He is earl."

At the mention of an earl, Penelope burst into tears.

Startled, Madame Zaborini looked up. She splayed her hands in the air and asked, "You no want fortune?"

Between little hiccups, Penelope managed to ask, "Will I marry this man?"

Madame Zaborini gave a deep, solemn nod.

Penelope only cried harder.

What was wrong with the girl? the gypsy wondered with a disgusted frown. She had told the silly creature what young women liked to hear. A tall dark stranger was in the future, perhaps an earl. But she was not pleased with the story. "What is wrong? You no like fortune?" the Romany woman demanded to know.

"I — I had hoped to marry someone else," Penelope sobbed on a muffled hiccup.

Madame Zaborini gave a shrug. She shook her head twice, then picked up the teacup to try again. "I see no one else," she said flatly.

"Well, that's because there isn't anyone else yet," Penelope retorted, thinking that the gypsy should have known that all along.

"Aah," the gypsy remarked pensively.

"But I had hoped you might see someone though," Penelope added on a hopeful note.

After a thoughtful moment of silence, Madame Zaborini asked, "What's wrong with the dark earl?"

"Nothing, I suppose. Except that I don't love him, and I had wanted to marry for love."

Madame Zaborini rolled her eyes in the direction of heaven and cursed in an evil tongue. Aiya! These foolish gorgios! What did they know of enjoying life? Aloud, she asked, "Then why marry him at all, little one?"

"I must. My brother insists."

"Your brother?"

"Yes. I'm not of age and he's my guardian. I must obey him."

This Madame Zaborini understood. Even a Romany girl was bound to obey her male relatives. But no Romany would destine a woman to misery; a Romany had to be free and if one's heart was in pain, there could be no freedom. "Is there no changing your brother's decision? I'm sure he doesn't want you to be unhappy. Why not tell him how you feel?"

"I can't. You see, there's going to be a generous marriage settlement and Ned, my brother, needs those funds desperately. Besides which, the earl is his oldest friend."

"Then tell the earl," prompted the gypsy.

"I don't want to hurt his feelings."

"Has the man said he loved you?" the gypsy asked, to which Penelope nodded no. The gypsy woman went on, "Then not to worry."

"But he's set on the match. You see, he lives miles away in the Highlands and was ever so lonely without a wife. I couldn't send him back there alone."

Aiya! That did it. If the foolish gorgio could not take good advice then there was no helping her. So much for honesty!

She would simply have to tell the girl what she wanted to hear. Once more she peered at the bottom of the cup. "Aiya! I see someone now. A man with blue eyes and light hair. There are two of them," she embellished. "Twins. But only one will win your heart."

"The dark earl isn't there?"

"No. He's gone."

"Oh, thank you!" Penelope clapped her hands at such promising news.

After paying Madame Zaborini, she left the caravan in high alt. Every step of the way to the town house on Hay's Mews she searched the crowds for a glimpse of fair twins. A young lady never knew when she might encounter her intended, and Penelope was determined to find her true love before Duncan Ramsey set a date for their wedding.

The air in the conservatory at Cockleshell Manse was humid. The heavy scent of moist earth mingled with the light perfume of gardenias and roses. Tina and Duncan Ramsey sat on wicker chairs beside the statue of a Greek muse poised above a pond where large orange coy circled between lily pads. Gold

Tabby perched at the edge of the pool with her kittens; they pawed at the fish. Behind them the children played with Black Jack, the green-winged macaw.

Ramsey looked at Tina. Her crown of glossy wine-colored hair was pulled to one side by a velvet ribbon that matched the violet hue of her eyes. He gave her a searching glance and said the one thing he had been dying to say all afternoon. "You must tell me about yourself."

At this directness, Tina gave a start. Duncan Ramsey was a perplexing man. This was his second visit to the Manse in less than a week's time, and his arrival had been as distinctly unsettling as the first. Tina was plagued by the question of why he had returned so soon. Certainly, it had not been for the purpose of joining them in the park and cavorting on the hobby horse with the boys as he had done. But what reason could it be? The terrible suspicion that he knew what the Council intended came to her. That was impossible, or at least she hoped it was, for she did not relish the thought of seeing her future once again laid open to Duncan Ramsey. She did not need anyone's assistance or pity. No matter what Mr. Bentham conjectured, it was likely — she had reasoned after a good night's sleep — nothing more than malicious threats on the part of Mrs. Chudleigh. Tina was certain she could convince the Council of the error of their judgment, and the trouble would be over before it really began.

In a voice that was not altogether steady, she replied, "There isn't a great deal to tell, my lord. I have had two homes. One here at Cockleshell Manse and the other in Devon at Ambleside with my grandfather."

"And your parents?"

Tina focused on a gardenia blossom. "I have no recall of them. They died of cholera while in Venice when I was a babe."

Detecting the reticence in her voice, he apologized. "I'm sorry. I didn't intend to talk about something that might cause you distress."

An unfamiliar saltiness prickled her eyes. "You did not know," she said aloud, while she thought, *My pain has nothing to do with my parents, it is you, my lord, and the anguish of discussing my past with you.* To put an end to this conversation, she said, "The sum of my existence has transpired within those two settings — Devon and Cockleshell Manse. It's a subject of little fascination, I assure you."

"What, no come-out?" he teased in an effort to make her smile. "No gay parties and endless lines of beaux waiting to sign your dance card? What about — " The unfinished sentence hung in the air between them. The only sound was her hard-caught breath. His eyes flew to her face. She was staring at him with naked anguish in those glorious eyes. It was a pain he had seen before, and he studied Tina with the grimmest expression as the memory of a skinny girl in an ill-fitting gown and their kiss in the cloakroom returned. Schooling his features to mask his astonishment, he could scarcely believe that the scrawny creature from Almack's had grown into such a lovely woman.

A distinctly sinking sensation enveloped Ramsey. It was as if he were facing death on the Peninsula and his every sin had come back to haunt him. He was the first to admit that he had been neither kind nor noble in his youth. He had been callow, arrogant, and supremely selfish. But he had never thought to come face-to-face with a past indiscretion as he was doing at this very moment. Hell and the Devil! No wonder Lady Christina had seemed familiar.

Ramsey had never recalled the girl's name, but he held the memory of her eyes — beautiful, wounded, and innocent eyes — through those dreadful months in Spain. Hers were the eyes that had haunted him in Vittoria and across the Pyrenees; the eyes that had come to him in the field hospital outside Bordeaux. Hers was the smile that he had seen when he searched his memory for an image of something free of death and mutilation.

Although he knew it was no excuse, he had been rowing with half an oar when Tweeddale and Durham had placed the wager: thirty pounds that he could not engage the sour-looking chit long enough to steal a kiss. It seemed an easy way to turn a profit. He had not considered the consequences of his actions; the girl had merely been a pawn. But when he had lied and said he had been watching her and she had responded with such trusting innocence, he had felt a kernel of reluctance. It was not often that Ramsey encountered goodness in his fast set, but he still recognized it, and there had been no denying that the girl was more than innocent, she was genuinely pure of heart and mind. While they were dancing he had spotted his friends and that spark of recalcitrance was stamped out. He had made a wager and must see the deed through or face humiliation, so he concentrated on that and nothing more.

Her laughter when the orchestra quickened its tempo had nearly breached the cynical armor that insulated the few scruples he possessed. Even now after all that time he could still see her flushed face framed by bouncing curls. In the end, though, it was the kiss that had been his undoing. Having never touched an innocent, he was unprepared for the sweetness of her lips and the trusting surrender when she opened her mouth beneath his. He would always remember the delicate scent of lavender and how she had tasted like the first clean breath of springtime. For a moment he had actually lost his wits. A quick kiss was bad enough, but to have felt the stirring of passion was another ball of wax. That had troubled him for months and when he lay on his cot at night trying to remember why they were fighting, he thought of the girl, but he could not recall her name.

Now what was he to do? Was he to calmly say, *Excuse me, Lady Christina, but I've just realized I'm the cad who seduced you for a wager?* That was a half-corked idea. Of course, he couldn't do that. What then? Evidently, she had recognized him. That explained why she had been so cool in the park. She had every right to loathe him. Verily, she must detest him. Yet for reasons of her own she had chosen to keep quiet. The only gentlemanly thing was to follow the lady's lead. He would not embarrass her by bringing up the past unless she did so first. An odd spasm tightened about his chest, the likes of which he had not experienced since that night when the girl with the immense round eyes had begged him not to apologize. It was nothing more than guilt, Ramsey was certain, just as he was certain that he owed a debt to Lady Christina both as her kinsman and as the man who had sorely misused her. It was a debt he willingly accepted, although at that moment he knew not how he might repay it.

Overhead the sulfur-crested cockatoo squawked as Black Jack chased it between the orange trees. The children clambered to the other side of the room, and Ramsey emerged from his reverie. Tina looked at him. She did not know how to answer his question, and in the next instant she forgot her own pain, for the expression in his eyes touched her heart. Of a sudden, the most incredible thought occurred to her: this man was cast adrift precisely as the children had been. An ironical smile lit her eyes, and as she might have taken in another stray cat, she invited, "Would you like to join us for dinner this evening, my lord?"

To Tina's astonishment, Duncan Ramsey, Earl of Croick, enthusiastically accepted.

Belowstairs Cook and Hobbins prepared a special meal in the earl's honor.

"Could scarce believe it when Lady Tina told me what Mr. Bentham said. Didn't I say 'twas nothing but terrible news when that Chudleigh woman showed her face?" declared Cook as she rotated a leg of mutton in the roasting range.

On the other side of the pantry, Hobbins was preparing a platter of boiled ham and candied carrots. "There's got to be something we can do to stop that nosy bunch of do-gooders. Ignorant is what they are. Don't know good from bad, is what I say."

"Far too kindly for her own sake is our Lady Tina," grumbled the old woman.

"Well, no use crying over spilt milk. 'Tis done and the thing for it is what are we going to do about it now?" Hobbins stared at his wife.

"As I be seeing it, she's got to get married," Cook said, as if finding a husband for Tina was no more complex than boiling water.

"But who would the girl marry?" the old man asked.

There was a long and exceedingly deliberate pause.

"Oh, Cook," he exclaimed as if he had discovered the King's ransom. "Are you thinking what I'm thinking?"

"Why not? He likes the young ones, he does, and that's what matters most. And we won't be forgetting, he has a title; the bloodlines are good; and he's not married, nor are his affections elsewhere engaged," said Cook, sounding like the veriest dowager of the beau monde arranging a suitable match for her heiress.

"I don't know," was Hobbins's thoughtful response, not daring to say that he suspected Lady Tina would rather burn the Manse to the ground than marry a gentleman she hardly knew. "Something ain't right between them. Have you noticed how she looks at him sometimes? Like she doesn't trust him."

"Girlishness. Nothing more," dismissed Cook.

"And how would you be knowing that?" His white brows arched with curiosity.

"Threw an apple in the hearth."

"Old woman, take care!" He wagged a finger at his wife. "You'll be frightening the young ones with your charms, if you don't watch out."

"Bosh! Ain't nothing harmful. Don't ye want to know what happened?"

Hobbins shrugged. "You'll tell me anyway."

" 'Twas a silent burning."

"And what does that mean?"

"The courtship be smooth. The ending happy."

"That don't account for her standoffishness."

There was a twinkle in the old servant's eye. "Nothing that a fresh groaning cake won't remedy." Then Cook scurried from the kitchen before Hobbins could ask anymore questions.

At midnight, the groaning cake was folded in a dishcloth and stuffed securely within the depths of Cook's cloak. It was her old Grannie's recipe. Made of rye flour, cinnamon, nutmeg, and cardamom, and baked with only one purpose in mind. Only two pieces had been served at dinner. One to Lady Tina; the other to Duncan Ramsey.

The waxing moon barely cast enough light to pick out the flat stones that paved the way to the churchyard in Bloomsbury. Cook moved through rising mist and when she reached her destination — a barren spot beneath an ash tree in the southeast corner of the hallowed ground — she dug a small hole. Into it she placed the groaning cake and a boiled egg, emptied of its meat and filled with salt. She stepped back from the hole, tossed in three handfuls of salt, then she turned around, faced the church, and chanted in broad West Country tones:

"Salt I throw, Salt that grow.
He that is to marry her,
Come after Lady Tina and sow."

★

The words bounced off the lichen-covered grave slabs and flew upward into the night. This charm had worked for West Country women since before the Conqueror. Cook had followed every requisite of the ancient rite; Lady Tina and the earl had both eaten from the same groaning cake; Cook had walked to the nearest and oldest graveyard beneath a crescent new moon to bury the uneaten cake. It would not fail. Before summer's end, Lady Tina and Duncan Ramsey would be married.

Five

"Hush up, you two," Joshua ordered beneath a cupped hand, but neither Finny nor Francis heard this admonition as they fidgeted in their seats.

Disorder was rampant in the schoolroom. Before departing the previous evening, the earl had promised to take the lads to the British Museum to view the Egyptian Hall, and as he was expected to arrive within the hour it was nigh on impossible for Finny and Francis to concentrate on anything other than the prospect of being in the same room with a score of two-thousand-year-old corpses.

A giggle erupted from the far end of the row, and Joshua set a chastising elder sibling stare upon Lettie whose demeanor was alternating between blushes and almost out-of-control giggles. Knowing that Lettie cared little for anything dead, Joshua shook his head, unable to comprehend what excuse she might own for being distracted from her studies.

Of course, it was no use Joshua wondering. No one but another female could understand Lettie's behavior; she was absorbed in highly romantic recollections of the earl's presence at their dinner table last evening.

Oh, how handsome he was, her thoughts began, *and how kind, how polite, how gentlemanly, nay how knightly he had been toward all of them, but especially to Tina mum.* Here the girl blushed anew, casting a glance at Lady Christina and continuing to muse, *Oh, how beautiful she was . . . as lovely as a princess. And oh, wouldn't it be perfect, wouldn't it be splendiferous for the earl to marry Lady Christina? Yes, that was what was going to happen.* Truth to tell, the earl did not want to take the boys to see some icky old pharaohs, rather he needed an excuse to come to Cockleshell Manse to see Tina mum. Lettie buried her face in Saxon history to muffle giggles of delight at the prospect of welcoming the earl into their family. Just think, she would wear a fancy gown with pastel lace about the hem and sleeves, and she would stand on the altar holding a basket of flowers that matched Tina mum's bridal bouquet. The flowers were bound to be lilies or roses at least, and there would be a great celebration with dancing and lemon cakes and marzipan pyramids. Oh, what a fine day it would be.

As for the female subject in this romantic whimsy, Lady Christina, too, was engrossed in thoughts of Duncan Ramsey. She stood before a mullioned schoolroom window gazing out upon the gravel drive oblivious of the goings-on about her. Inviting Duncan Ramsey for dinner had been an eye-opening experience, and Tina could not stop reflecting how unlike he was from the officer she had encountered five years before. The Duncan Ramsey who had sat at the head of her table had been sensitive to Joshua's need to be treated like a man rather than a schoolboy and to Lettie's budding feminine insecurities; he had even, she suspected, been aware of her misgivings and had gone to some effort to minimize any awkward silent moments. Yes, he was much changed, she admitted, unable to prevent the irregular fluttering of her heart when she recalled how he had blended into their family gathering. Most unmarried gentlemen did not enjoy the exuberant company of other people's children, but if this was true of Duncan Ramsey, he had well disguised any displeasure. Indeed, there was nothing about the way he had joined in the jovial conversation to make an observer think he was a stranger to their table. He had wanted to be there, and it seemed like the most natural occurrence to have him sitting at the head of the table as if it were his proper place.

His proper place.

The thought was a jolting one, and it caused Tina's heart to skip a beat, for of a sudden, she realized something about herself that she had conveniently denied.

Despite the children's love, and Cook's and Hobbins's devotion, she suffered from a certain kind of loneliness that could be assuaged by nothing other than the presence of a gentleman. Oh yes, she was content, but Ramsey had reminded her of the companionable dinners she used to enjoy with Grandfather. The earl had reminded her of the dream she had once owned of being wife and companion to the man she loved, and last evening had been unbearably close to that dream. Long ago she had closed her eyes and seen herself seated at one end of a table, a gentleman in the opposite seat and healthy children all around them; there had been affable chatter and shared pleasure in the children's antics, and there had been love in the gentleman's eyes as he smiled at the children, their children. Now she closed her eyes, and she saw Duncan Ramsey in that seat and he was smiling warmly around the table, and a strange little pain tightened about her chest.

The earl reminded Tina that although she had succeeded as an independent woman in managing her own affairs, independence had certain drawbacks. Isolation. Loneliness. Uncertainty. It was frightening to think that having been given the freedom to make her own choices she might have made the wrong ones; choices so misguided that she might lose everything that meant anything to her. Too, it was frightening to consider that Duncan Ramsey, who had played so great a role in the direction of the life she had chosen, would be the very person to shake her convictions. It was even more alarming to realize that she wished for more evenings like the one last night, and with that thought the foundation of her entire existence seemed to weaken.

Opening her eyes, she turned away from the mullioned window to observe the children. They were a family, the children were hers in every way except for blood, and things were fine the way they were, weren't they? No matter what the Council said or how her traitorous mind waxed poetic about Duncan Ramsey, she had made the right choices, and she did not need anything or anyone else. Or did she?

How her sensible heart and logical mind could have been so completely boggled by Duncan Ramsey was a mystery to Tina, and she needed time to sort out her feelings. Thank goodness she had declined the earl's invitation to visit the museum; a quiet after-noon of reflection, perhaps a walk in the park, was how she intended to pass the afternoon.

From a preselected vantage point in the kitchen garden Cook espied the tall gentle-man as he made his way down the drive toward Cockleshell Manse. She was not really picking brussels sprouts, and as soon as the earl rapped upon the door with his gold-tipped cane, she quit the garden. Taking immense satisfaction in his arrival, she pro-ceeded to the great hall, where she hovered near Hobbins while he took the gentleman's beaver hat and coat.

"Pleased to be seeing ye, I am, yer lord-ship." She scurried forward and gave a proper curtsy, all the while making every effort to avoid the reproachful glares that Hobbins cast her way.

"I'm pleased to be back, Cook," the earl replied in a cordial tone of voice. "That was an excellent meal you prepared last evening."

"Thank you, my lord," put in Hobbins, endeavoring to direct his wife away from the earl, but she paid not the slightest notice. What maggot had infested her aged brain Hobbins could not fathom; nevertheless, he knew it boded no good and he wished she would retire to the pantry or nursery, where she would be out of harm's way.

Not to be deterred, Cook pursued the men down the corridor. "And what might be bringing ye out to Cockleshell Manse so early in the day?" she demanded in a manner far too familiar for one of her station.

The old woman's unseemly behavior did not offend Ramsey, and he grinned at her. It was comforting to know Lady Christina and her brood were guarded over by so imposing a female. "The lads talked so much of the Egyptian exhibit I thought they would appreciate a chance to observe the relics firsthand."

Cook returned his grin. The earl might be thinking he had returned because of the lads, but she knew otherwise. He had returned because the groaning cake was working its magic.

"Are they finished with their morning lessons?" he asked Hobbins upon entering the library.

"Not much longer, I don't be guessing, they'll be," put in Cook before Hobbins might speak. "Can I get ye some refreshment while ye be waiting, yer lordship?" She was eager for the opportunity to slip a pinch of powdered briony root in his cup.

"Some of that delicious cocoa would be nice."

Giving a nod, Cook shuffled off to the

pantry well pleased with the progress of her scheme. In all likelihood, briony root was not necessary, but as it would do no harm and every little bit would help to speed along a happily-ever-after ending for Lady Tina, Cook did not hesitate to add several pinches to the pot of cocoa. She set the tortoiseshell glazed pot upon a silver tray beside two cups and saucers — one for the earl, the other for Lady Tina — then gave the tray to Hobbins who carried it up to the unsuspecting soon-to-be bridegroom.

Settling back in a wing chair by the fire, Ramsey enjoyed a long sip of the sweet frothy liquid. It was a shame Lady Christina would not be joining them this afternoon; he could not deny the pleasure he experienced in her company, particularly watching her affection-ate interaction with the children. The fact was that while watching Lady Christina with the children his soul was nourished in some unknown and inexplicable fashion.

It was an unsettling conclusion, and if that was not odd enough, it was accompanied by piercing guilt when he considered the plea-sure he had found at her dinner table. His conscience argued it was wrong to derive the merest iota of warmth or satisfaction from Lady Christina. Already he had robbed her of trust and hope, and it was his duty to determine the best way to repay his debt to her, not to linger about her home in the hopes of being included in family activities.

The library door opened, drawing him from this troublesome reverie, and he turned upon the upholstered seat to see who was about to enter.

Hobbins stood on the threshold and announced in creaking tones, "Mr. Horace Cadwallader."

In walked Mr. Cadwallader dressed to the nines in a narrow-waisted coat of canary yellow and tight, yellow and black striped trousers; an extravagant arrangement of neckcloth, varnished black boots, and a quizzing glass on a length of yellow silk completed the ensemble. He looked like some dandy out for an afternoon strut in Piccadilly. At the sight of another man in the room Cadwallader stopped in his tracks so abruptly that the quizzing glass popped from its precarious position in his right eye socket to dangle from the silken rope about his neck.

The earl stood and extended a hand. "Duncan Ramsey," he introduced himself, neglecting to mention his title.

But Cadwallader knew the identity of the gentleman right away. Even middle-class merchants had heard of Duncan Ramsey, notorious rake, gambler, and war hero, and

Cadwallader could not help thinking how the presence of so infamous a gentleman at Cockleshell Manse would turn Agatha Chudleigh on her ear.

"Won't you join me in a cup of chocolate?" inquired the earl. "We've a while yet to wait. Lady Christina is finishing the children's morning lessons."

"Most considerate of you." Cadwallader took the opposite seat and helped himself to a cup of cocoa.

Ramsey eyed Cadwallader, blatant curiosity etched upon his features. He had often heard the man's name bantered about his club in connection with business ventures, but this overdressed peacock was not what he had expected when envisioning a self-made man from London's docks. This walking stick in daffodil was an enigma, and of a sudden, Ramsey found himself entertaining a host of decidedly proprietary questions. How did Lady Christina come to be acquainted with someone of his reputation? What was the nature of their relationship? Did he visit Cockleshell Manse often?

"Have you known Lady Christina long?" Ramsey asked with the tilt of one black brow.

"Since the first of the year when I moved into Park Village East."

"You're neighbors then?"

"Yes."

The earl gave a sharp nod. Neighbors. That made sense. But *why* was he calling upon Lady Christina when there was no chaperon present? Where in the blazes was the man's wife? Never one to beat about the proverbial bush, he inquired, "And how does Mrs. Cadwallader like her new home?"

"There is no Mrs. Cadwallader." He took another sip of hot cocoa, wondering why this gentleman displayed so possessive an air regarding Lady Christina. After another sip, he set aside the cup to raise the quizzing glass. One grossly magnified eye surveyed Ramsey. "And how long have *you* known the lady?"

"I'm a relative of Lady Christina's. Third cousins, to be exact, and in a manner of speaking you could say I'm her guardian."

At this intelligence Horace Cadwallader's face lit up as if he had won the grand national lottery, and he rushed into speech, "Glad to meet you, sir. Most glad, indeed, for I'm calling today with a specific purpose in mind. You would be the gentleman to whom one addresses one's suit for the lady?"

Ramsey leaned forward in the chair. Had he understood correctly? Was Horace Cadwallader here to offer his hand in matrimony to Lady Christina? If so, that might explain the preposterous outfit he was sporting; men were known to commit all manner of folly when in the throes of love.

"No doubt you're surprised, sir, and I understand your reaction, for I'm not a gentleman. Admittedly, I'm rough around the edges. Not the sort of husband a relative would want for the likes of Lady Christina, but my intentions are honorable."

Honorable or not, Ramsey did not like what he was hearing, and although he knew it was none of his business, he could not detour the direction of his thoughts. Wasn't Lady Christina's life fine just the way it was? What did she need with a man like Horace Cadwallader? Truth to tell, he could not suppress the lamentable conclusion that the lady did not need any man. She already had wealth and security, and a nursery of little ones. Why would she want to leg-shackle herself to any man?

Speaking with the utmost dignity, Cadwallader continued, "I would never dare, nay presume, to offer for a lady of superior rank were the situation not of the most urgent nature. My offer is intended to protect and save the lady." To this provocative statement, suspicion flared upon Ramsey's countenance, whereupon the entrepreneur's ears turned a vivid shade of scarlet. Waving his bony hands in denial, Cadwallader hastened to add, "Oh, no! Not *that*. Please do not misunderstand. I haven't been courting the lady and there's nothing of an an — " he gave an awkward cough, then pursed his lips in frustration " — of an intimate nature between us. Oh, I'm making a devil of a tangle out of this, aren't I?"

Taking pity on the man, Ramsey suggested, "Perhaps you would do best to begin at the beginning."

"Quite right." Whereupon Cadwallader proceeded to explain about the Park Village East Council of Concerned Property Owners and its resolution to force Lady Christina to adhere to its rules of conduct. "But upon consideration, sir, I've come to a parting of ways with the Council, and I'd like to help the lady. She's done nothing wrong. Fact is, what she's done for the children is most commendable. So, having cogitated upon the predicament, it seems marriage would be the most sensible solution. There's no way Mrs. Chudleigh could argue with that or with me, don't you agree?"

It appeared the lady did need a gentleman after all, and Ramsey could not help smiling. Horace Cadwallader had shown him the way to repay his debt to Lady Christina. "The obvious solution is not always the best. You said this so-called Citizens Council was under the impression Lady Christina has no male relatives. Evidently, they're unaware of my existence." His smile widened as his sense of purpose solidified. He would do everything within his power to guarantee the Council's failure; he would retain the services of the finest solicitors; he would protect Lady Christina and her family; he would preserve the unique way of life she had made for them. It was the perfect scheme to repay his debt to Lady Christina. "Mayhap informing the Council of my frequent presence would suffice."

Mr. Cadwallader rubbed his chin and gave the matter some thought. "It might work, but on the other hand, they're an angry lot, my lord, spiteful, in fact, and I'm not sure they'll settle for anything other than victory. Particularly Mrs. Chudleigh, when she hears your name."

"My name?"

"Don't mean to be impertinent, your lordship, but I recognized your name straightaway. You're the Earl of Croick, and even before you inherited you've long been on the top of Mrs. Chudleigh's list of the intemperate and degenerate. Woman's got a terrible moral bee in her bonnet and it might be you'd worsen Lady Christina's quandary."

It had never occurred to Ramsey that anyone other than the social sticklers of Mayfair cared one whit for his jaded past. Nor had it occurred to him that association with him might taint a blood relative. It appeared that his model conduct these past months was to little avail, and tragically, Lady Christina would continue to be a victim of his sordid past.

Before Ramsey might pursue the issue, the children burst into the room followed by Lady Christina. She was radiant in a simple round gown trimmed with lavender-colored velvet that matched the color of her eyes. Not a trace of inner nervousness was revealed in the welcoming smile she bestowed upon her visitors.

"Good day, gentlemen," she greeted in a clear, gentle voice. In turn, the children lined up to make their bows and curtsies.

Moments later Cook entered with the lad's cloaks, and as fate would have it she noticed a cup of hot chocolate poised at Horace Cadwallader's lips. Emitting a strangled cry, she swooned into a dead faint upon the red Herat carpet.

The better part of the next forty-five minutes was devoted to reviving Cook. It was no easy feat. Each time the woman opened her eyes and focused upon Mr. Cadwallader she began to swoon anew, pointed a finger in his direction, and groaned, "Not him. Oh, no, not him. Not him."

Divining that it would be best to depopulate the premises, Ramsey directed the children into the corridor, decided to include Lettie and Molly on the outing, and having made quick work of locating the girls' bonnets, he led the children forth to view the antiquities at the British Museum.

"That was most peculiar," Tina remarked to Mr. Cadwallader once Hobbins, who was not behaving in a remotely sympathetic fashion, had ushered his wife from the library. "Cook has never behaved like that before. I can't imagine what overset her so."

Acting for all the world like a truant schoolboy, Mr. Cadwallader shifted his weight from one booted foot to the other. "You're a gracious lady to pretend it wasn't my fault." He raised a hand to prevent Tina from interrupting. "I do not blame the woman in the least, for she must treasure you as a daughter and upon my previous visits to your home I was less than neighborly."

"Ah yes." Impossible though it might seem Tina had momentarily forgotten the Council's threat to take the children from her. A chill crept into her voice. "What is it the Council wishes this time, sir? What message have you for me?"

"I do not come on Council business, my lady. Indeed, I've divorced myself from their intentions. What you said the other day put me to reflecting, and I'd be a blind fool and cruel into the bargain not to support your efforts to give those children a better life. I never had much of a childhood myself, and when I think of what you're doing . . . when I see them running and singing in the park instead of crying from the hunger and beatings and loneliness . . . then I know there's no denying you're an angel, and I want to help you, my lady. Indeed, I've pledged myself to solving this predicament. No matter what it takes."

"That's wonderful news, Mr. Cadwallader." A spark of hope illuminated her eyes as she sat upon the chair Ramsey had occupied. "I must tell you that I've already consulted with my solicitor and he wasn't encouraging. Mr. Bentham believes that as long as the Council intends to take action against me it's conceivable they may succeed. Do you think you could convince them to cease their action?"

"Regrettably, I've already tried and failed."

A little gasp of disappointment escaped her lips. "Oh, no, that's terrible. Have you any other ideas?"

"Yes. One." He coughed, again shifted his weight from foot to foot, and then fiddled with the high starched collar of his fancy white shirt. "I was wondering if you'd consider . . . that is to say, I would be honored, Lady Christina, to make you my wife."

Tina looked upon Mr. Cadwallader with an air of stark amazement. His proposal was astounding, but its implication was even more remarkable. No matter what Grandfather had intended, no matter how she had managed thus far, the edicts of Society would prevail; ultimately, marriage was the only course for all females, and Lady Christina Braughton was no longer exempt. Even Mr. Cadwallader, a man who had built an empire from nothing, did not think a female on her own could prevail against odds such as she faced. Coming so close on those revealing thoughts about Duncan Ramsey, this development produced a profoundly disheartening effect upon Tina. Several moments passed and still she was robbed of the ability to speak.

"You're shocked and rightly so, my lady. I'm the first to admit I'm no gentleman, but I'd be a loyal husband and a decent father to the children, and with a man, a husband, at Cockleshell Manse I believe the Council would cease to have grounds for any complaint."

"Oh, dear sir, it's not you that causes me to react with such shock, but the entire proposition. You see, I can't help but be appalled by the notion that there's no way I can continue to live my own life, that I must marry and give up the independence my grandfather granted me."

"I did not mean to distress you in any way, Lady Christina. It was my intention to provide you a foil against the Council, and should you accept my offer you would not have to give up your independence or control of your own monies. Ours would be naught but a marriage of convenience. I wouldn't dare to impose upon you in any way, my lady."

"Sir, you say you are no gentleman, but I disagree. What you offer is most gallant and gentlemanly. Still I must turn down your proposal." For one moment, she feared he was about to fall to his knees before her, and quickly she expanded, "It would not be fair, sir, for I do not love you. You see, having always wished to marry for love I do not think I would be a tolerable wife otherwise, and you, sir, are a man who deserves more. There's another reason as well. Being of a somewhat stubborn disposition, it's my firm intention to resolve this matter on my own . . . with a little help from persons such as you, of course."

"I understand, but please, don't close the door on my offer. You must promise to come to me for help at any time." On an afterthought, he amended, "That is, if you need it."

She smiled. "I promise."

"And please, I would be honored if you would consider me a friend, for I shall champion your cause in any way I might."

"Thank you, sir. I accept your offer of friendship." She stood. Their interview was at an end, and she extended her hand in farewell.

Upon Mr. Cadwallader's departure, Tina left for that walk in the park. It was the best way she knew to clear her head and consider the serious issue before her. But no matter how she tried she could not concentrate on the Council while images of Duncan Ramsey intruded upon her thoughts. The Council's threats were bad enough, and that man could not have found a worse time to step back into her life. Nothing seemed right anymore. Until a few days ago her seclusion had seemed idyllic, but now seclusion became isolation, and solitude became loneliness.

"Lady Christina?"

Glancing up, Tina saw the epitome of a well-bred aristocratic beauty seated in an open carriage. "Yes?"

"I trust I did not frighten you," the young lady said, her sweet voice laced with the hint of an Irish brogue.

"No," Tina replied, a trifle disconcerted, for the truth was she had not heard the carriage, nor had she expected to encounter anyone in the park.

"Don't you remember me? I'm Mina Cavendish. We met last fall at Gunter's."

Her memory jogged, Tina recalled their previous meeting. "Of course, I remember. How nice it is to see you again." In celebration of Lettie's birthday, Tina had taken her and the boys to the famed confectioner's tearoom beneath the sign of the pineapple at Number 7, Berkeley Square. The merry September afternoon had been made even more enjoyable when a beautiful lady at a nearby table joined their festivities. Confessing to having been the lone girl in a household of boys, the lady had charmed the lads with tales of her siblings' birthday antics, and in turn, she had made Lettie feel quite grown up by sharing sisterly confidences with her. Then as the children had settled down to a feast of flavored ices and petits fours frosted with pink and yellow butter cream, the young lady had engaged in congenial chatter with Tina. How pleasant it had been to spend an hour with someone her own age, and Tina had not forgotten a single detail of that splendid afternoon at Gunter's. "You're the Countess of Brierly."

The countess laughed. "Only in the most formal of circumstances. Please, call me Mina. All my friends do and I had hoped that we might become friends, but I haven't seen you about Town since that time. I suppose you must be busy with that delightful family."

"Quite so and we've grown by one."

"That's wonderful news. Oh, do come sit up here and tell me the whole of it."

Tina accepted the footman's assistance to climb into the barouche and sit beside the countess.

"Tell me, is it another boy or a girl, and how did this little one come to be a part of your household?" the young countess inquired, scooting over to make room for Tina.

"She's a girl, and she was simply left on our doorstep."

"How remarkable." Upon their previous encounter Mina had been fascinated by Lady Christina; such independence coupled with genuine compassion was rare in a lady. The countess had been drawn to Lady Christina, for she had seen much of herself in the vivacious young woman who dared to defy society's expectations of a lady of rank. "And what else have you been doing?"

"The children keep me busy. There are school lessons each morning and outings when the weather permits. Lettie has begun to play the pianoforte, and Joshua is preparing to attend Rugby next term."

A small frown creased the countess's brow. "Do you often walk in the park?"

"Yes, when I need to think."

"And today there was something weighing upon your mind." She patted Tina's hand in understanding. "Ah, well, if that's the case then it was destiny that we should meet again this afternoon, for I'm an excellent listener."

Tina was taken aback. "I could not trouble you with my worries."

"But that's what friends are for. And you need not worry about gossip. I'm the soul of discretion and would never divulge the confidence of a friend."

This was said with such genuine kindness that Tina could not refuse the offer, and shyly, she explained her predicament with the Council and Mr. Cadwallader's proposal.

At length, the countess remarked, "It sounds as if you need to get out more often on your own and more than simply a walk in the park. I don't mean to diminish the gravity of the situation, but I've always found that if you distance yourself from your problems then it's easier to consider them objectively."

"I had not thought of that. It does make sense."

The countess gave a self-satisfied nod. "My husband and I are having a small gathering in about ten days. It would be the perfect way to get away from your worries. Say you'll come."

"It does sound like a good idea, but I'm not sure — "

"Nonsense. You can't refuse me."

Tina glanced down at the folds of her green pelisse. How was she to explain that there was more to her hesitation than not feeling right about turning her back on her problems? There was also the notion of ending her isolation from Society, and that was most frightening to consider. Friendship with the countess was one thing, but a social gathering was another matter altogether. What if someone recognized her? What if they remembered her failed Season? *Never took* was what the gossips had said, and Tina did not relish the prospect of again being made to feel like an azalea bush that had failed to root. Or worse, what if there was such a round of gossip that Ramsey realized who she was? That, for reasons of which she was not certain, was something she did not wish to face. Not on top of everything else. Too much was changing, too swiftly, and she was not certain if it was wise to accept the invitation at the risk of causing more disruptions in her life.

"Now don't refuse me," Mina said with a pretty smile of encouragement. "It's going to be a small group and not in the least bit fashionable at that, for the Season's not yet begun. My husband's sister, Catherine, and my brother, Liam, are returning from their wedding trip, and we did so want to do a little something in their honor. It shall be a few old friends and immediate family. That's who I was visiting just now — one of my brothers lives on the other side of the park."

If it was to be nothing more than family and close friends, there could be no harm in accepting the invitation. What could happen? "Thank you for your kind offer. I should be delighted to attend," Tina replied, never suspecting that the Countess of Brierly was speculating upon which of her brothers would appeal to Lady Christina. Of the four O'Kieffe brothers, two remained bachelors: Michael, the softhearted one, who was perpetually rescuing ladies in distress, and Kevin, who preferred fallen ladies of the ton.

"Excellent," said Mina, having decided that Michael was the most likely candidate. "I'll send a footman round in the morning with an invitation. Oh, my dear, don't look so apprehensive. You'll have a splendid time, I promise, and who knows who you might encounter." The Countess of Brierly was a notorious romantic, and there was no way a single lady or gentleman could escape her matrimonial machinations.

The carriage arrived at the gates of Cockleshell Manse, and the countess directed the coachman to the end of the drive.

"Won't you come in for tea?" inquired Tina. "The children are soon to return from an outing and would love to see you again."

"Not today, thank you. May I call another time?"

"Of course. Visitors are always welcome at Cockleshell Manse."

"You know, I think we shall be friends after all." The countess gave Tina's hand a cordial squeeze. "Don't you agree?"

"I do," she replied as she stepped down from the carriage. "I'm most pleased to have encountered you today."

"Good. I'll come to call soon and bring my husband's grandmother, the dowager countess. *Grandmère's* prodigiously clever, y'know, and I'm sure she'll have an idea how to solve your predicament. As kind as this Mr. Cadwallader may be, you're quite right to refuse his offer. And *Grandmère* would agree. You mustn't marry him. You must never marry for anything but love." She paused an instant before asking, "Is there no one who holds your affection?"

"No one," Tina answered despite the troubling image of Duncan Ramsey's lean tanned face that flashed before her mind's eye.

"We'll have to remedy that. Mayhap you shall like one of my brothers or one of my husband's friends. Who knows?" With all the air of someone who knows from personal experience, Mina concluded, "Love is generally found in the most unexpected places."

Six

Cook had to hide the white and gold chrysanthemums before Lady Christina returned
from her walk. It was bad enough that Mr.
Cadwallader had finished an entire cup of
cocoa laced with briony root, but to allow
Lady Christina to receive his flowers would be
courting further disaster. There was no telling
how she might react to the flowers. Having
never received a bouquet from a gentleman,
her excitement was likely to be boundless,
and the last thing Cook wanted was Lady
Christina doing anything, however innocent,
to encourage the man before she had the occasion to reverse the effects of the briony root.

Hearing a carriage outside, the old woman
pushed the card down between the stems,
then glanced about the great hall in search of
a hiding place. She spotted a circular table
draped with a length of magenta velvet and
positioned in the alcove beneath the bend in
the staircase. It was a perfect place to which to
relegate something one wished did not exist in

the first place, and Cook scurried toward the table.

The front door opened. "Cook, whatever are you doing?" inquired Tina as she took off her bonnet and set it on a nearby console along with her gloves.

Cook jumped away from the table, and the cloth fell back in place. Her tone was heavy with feigned confusion. "Doing, my lady?"

"Yes, what are you doing? It appears you're hiding flowers beneath that table, and I'd like to know why." Tina crossed the great hall, reached beneath the table, and pulled out the massive but tasteful arrangement of white and gold chrysanthemums mixed with china asters upon a bed of variegated ivy.

"Putting them in a safe place is what I'm about, for ye know how wild the children are when they return from an outing, dashing about like a tribe of Welshmen. 'Tis not wanting the flowers to be upset, I be."

The skeptical expression upon Tina's face was full proof that she did not believe a word of this explanation, but not wishing to argue with the woman, who had been acting in a most peculiar fashion all day, she pretended to accept it. She set the arrangement on top of the circular table. "Where did they come from?"

"They were delivered while ye were on yer

walk," came Cook's reluctant and uninformative answer.

"Oh, how I love surprises," exclaimed Tina, failing to notice in the throes of her elation the fierce scowl that was settling upon Cook's ancient face. "Who do you suppose sent them?"

The old woman's disapproving expression deepened. She fibbed, "I'm sure I couldn't be saying."

"But where's the card? There must have been a card." Tina parted the stems and delved into the ivy until she found what she was searching for. "Here it is, and look, oh, my gracious, you'll never believe this. They're from Mr. Cadwallader. How thoughtful of him. Listen to what he said: *Good Luck to a Lady Who Deserves Nothing but the Finest, From Your Loyal Servant, Neighbor and Friend.*"

"Harrumph." Cook had no intention of uttering a single positive syllable about the flowers, no matter how attractive they were, nor about the message, no matter how considerate it was, if they were from *that man*. "And why might Mr. Cadwallader be sending ye flowers, I'll be asking? 'Tis more the behavior of a suitor than a troublemaker."

"You're quite right. Oh, not that he's a suitor, but that Mr. Cadwallader is not a troublemaker. He's a friend, and just this afternoon he informed me of his decision to part ways with the Council, and he tendered his assistance to foil their purpose. In fact, he actually proposed to me."

"He what?" Cook's voice rose several octaves. Sweet heavens, disaster was looming on the horizon just as surely as the tapping of a death watch beetle augured dire misfortune. Oh, how was she to convince Mr. Cadwallader that it was in his best interest to eat an entire overcooked poppy seed cake at one sitting? Or how, if that did not work, might she induce him to swim in the Thames beneath a half-moon during a rainfall? Whatever method she employed to reverse the briony root, it had to occur before the next moon. "Do not be saying he proposed to ye."

"Yes, he proposed marriage. 'Twas a way to thwart the Council and not an altogether bad idea at that." Observing the color drain from the older woman's complexion, she added, "Oh, you mustn't be so shocked, dear Cook. Of course, I turned him down. You know I shall never marry for any reason save love." She picked up the flowers and held them at arm's length. "Nonetheless the flowers are exquisite. I believe I'll put them in the library. They'll look perfect on the pianoforte. Don't you agree?"

"Yes, my lady," muttered Cook, still uncertain that Mr. Cadwallader did not represent a potential calamity. "And would ye be liking a spot of tea?"

"Please. And bring enough for the children and the earl. I imagine they'll be back at any moment and shall no doubt be ravenous."

In the library, Tina made an unnecessary fuss over the flowers. Although they were perfect the way they were, she could not resist moving them in tiny increments from one end of the pianoforte to the other, stepping back with each repositioning to decide which spot would show them off to their fullest advantage. In her concentration, she did not hear the door open and was surprised when the earl came to stand beside her, the children entering the room in his wake.

"Hello, my lord." She glanced up at him with a delightful sparkle in her eyes, and a smile curved upon her lips as the unexpected thought struck Tina that she was glad to see Duncan Ramsey. Much had happened this day, and although none of it — neither Mr. Cadwallader's gallant offer of assistance, nor the renewal of her acquaintance with the Countess of Brierly — was bad, it was all quite out of the ordinary. She felt as if she were in a racing curricle, speeding across the countryside and unable to focus on the passing hayricks and sheep. Much had happened and with such swiftness that she had not had time to digest it, and that was a most unsettling state of affairs. Somehow, at this moment, Duncan Ramsey represented the familiar, and that was comforting. Her smile deepened. "How was the outing?"

"Stupendous! Top-drawer!" chimed Finny and Francis.

"The cat's meow!" said Joshua.

"Pluperfect in every way," was Lettie's restrained, but indisputably stellar reply.

The earl concurred. "Yes, it was a smashing success, if five utterly exhausted children, who consumed a full baker's dozen of hot buns and nigh on a gallon of lemonade, and claimed to have walked a distance equal to a round trip on the Brighton Road, and lastly, found the energy to extract the promise of a future outing via barge to Hampton Court, are a reasonable measure to go by."

"Faith, I would agree. All are certain signs of a high success. Thank you, sir, it was most generous of you." She sat upon the settee and began to pour a cup of tea for the earl. "I do hope you were not overly put upon. Their enthusiasm can be a tad unbridled at times, I fear."

"It was my pleasure." He accepted the cup and took a seat in one of the winged chairs.

"As you're aware, I was an only child and did not enjoy the company of siblings, and though I'm told a large family is often the bain of more than one lad's childhood, it was a regrettable gap in mine. Today, I must confess to having relived some of my childhood, and I fear I may have been equally as unbridled as my charges." He chortled. "I had been to the exhibit only once before, and it's a wholly unique experience to view it with such candid companions. I had almost forgotten that dead bugs are much more precious than rubies."

"But that's not all that happened, Tina mum," Lettie said in excitement as she perched beside Lady Christina.

"It's not?"

"Yes, something very important happened."

"And what was that?"

"After the mummies we saw the Elgin Marbles."

The other children crowded round Tina, a portion of the tale spilling forth from each of them in turn.

"But the marbles weren't half as interesting as the mummies."

"Nothing more than slabs of stone."

"So when Molly got fidgety the earl told us some Greek myths."

"And we agreed upon a name for Baby."

"Diana Hunter Braughton," announced Lettie. "That is, of course, if you like it, too."

"It's a beautiful name." Tina put an arm about Lettie's shoulders, kissed her forehead and gave her a hug. "Of course, I like it, but I don't follow how Elgin Marbles and Greek myths arrive at Diana Hunter."

"Oh, that's easy," said Lettie. "You see, there was a Greek goddess named Artemis. She was the goddess of the hunt, and the earl said that the Greek people believed she protected all young living things."

Finny expanded, "Since someone protected Baby we thought it might have been Artemis, who brought her safely through the woods to Cockleshell Manse, and maybe we ought to name Baby after Artemis."

"It seemed like a good idea," Francis continued. "But then we agreed it wasn't a pretty enough name even if it did belong to a goddess."

Joshua concluded, "Then the earl told us the Romans called Artemis Diana. We decided that Diana was just right."

"And we thought that since it was the earl who told us about Artemis and Diana that he ought to be her godfather. Can he?" asked Lettie, the other children taking up the request in a pitch of high excitement.

"I . . . " Tina hesitated no more than a second, for the eager looks upon their young faces told her that no matter what she wished there could be only one response. "Of course, he may, if that's his wish."

"And can we have a grand party and a baptism like we did for Mary Katherine?"

"Yes."

The earl spoke up, "It was not my intention to intrude, and I will understand, if you would rather not — "

Tina did not let him continue. "Don't say another word, my lord, for it would break the children's hearts, if either of us were to naysay their plans. If you wish, there's no reason why you shouldn't stand as godfather," she said, but could think of any number of reasons why it was not a wise notion. First and foremost, there was the permanence it implied. Less than a month ago, Duncan Ramsey had been a vague and painful memory, and now he was to be a tangible part of the future. The prospect was an uneasy one. Sooner or later he would remember their previous encounter in the cloakroom at Almack's and then what would happen? Would he look upon her with pity or scorn or distaste? Sooner or later he would hear of the Council and its intent, and when that happened would she be forced to relinquish some of her independence to him?

The children, oblivious to her reluctance,

rejoiced over the favorable developments, finished their tea, and then retired to the second floor to ready for an early bedtime.

"What spectacular flowers," remarked the earl, casting about for something to say. "You must have been quite busy while we were away."

"Although I'd like to claim such talents, I must confess I'm not responsible for them. They were sent to me this afternoon, and in fact, they're the first I've ever received from a gentleman."

At this revelation Ramsey felt a sensation in his chest that he was unable to identify. Was it compassion? Or was it owing to a protective instinct? he mused as he recalled the purpose behind Horace Cadwallader's visit. Aloud, he speculated, "They're from a secret admirer?"

"An admirer, yes, but not a secret one. They're from my neighbor, Mr. Cadwallader."

"Oh." The earl could not help wondering if Cadwallader had proposed to Lady Christina, and if so, what her response had been. He fished about for more information. "Are they in celebration of a special occasion?"

"No."

"I see," he replied, wishing that she might be more forthcoming. Of a sudden, he stood, walked to the hearth, and stared at the blue-gold flames. His curiosity about Cadwallader's visit was intense, and he turned back to Lady Christina. "Mr. Cadwallader is a special friend?"

"Indeed, he is," she said with a smile that was far too brilliant for the earl's liking.

Ramsey wanted to ask, *Is that all?* but he dared not, sufficing instead to confine his next remark to a simple, "It's always nice to have a friend."

Tina nodded, and a short silence ensued, broken at last by the chimes of the corner tall clock striking six times.

Again, the earl stared into the flames. Was this the time to broach the issue of the Council and to offer his assistance? No, it was too soon. She was a proud and independent lady, and given their sordid past, she might very well misinterpret his motivations. It would be far better to win her trust, to become a friend, and then confront the problem. In the meantime, he could make some discreet queries on his own, perhaps hire an investigator to delve into the matter.

He faced Lady Christina. "It is late, and I must be going, but I look forward to my next outing with the children."

"As they do, I'm sure."

"You do not mind that I agreed to take them to Hampton Court without first asking your permission?"

"Not in the least." She was taken aback by the sudden restraint in his voice. Yes, he was a changed man, and although she did not understand why, she knew that he was neither as invulnerable nor as stalwart as he might wish to appear. And just as she had issued the dinner invitation last evening, Tina's warm-hearted nature compelled her to say, "You are always welcome in our home, my lord Ramsey."

Pleased that Lady Christina's willingness to have him at Cockleshell Manse would enable him to monitor developments regarding the Council, the earl smiled as he retrieved his cane from its resting place against the winged chair. "I shall check my engagement book before selecting a day for the outing, then I'll send a note round. Please let me know if the date is convenient for the children."

"Of course," was the extent of Tina's reply as she walked with the earl to the great hall and bid him farewell.

Later that evening, following a simple meal in her sitting room, Tina stole downstairs for one final peek at the flowers from Mr. Cadwallader. The fire had been damped, the lamps and tapers extinguished for the night, and the only light in the room was the faint golden glow that emanated in an arc about the hooded hearth. Tina crossed to the pianoforte and picked up the flowers, then set them on a table at the edge of the light. It was too bad that they would not last forever, but the friendship they symbolized would, and with that knowledge a sense of well-being encircled Tina.

Despite the uncertainty she faced, Tina had the resolve to confront whatever the future held, and she knew that her inner fortitude was not owing entirely to herself. This day, she had found two friends — Horace Cadwallader and the Countess of Brierly — and in accepting their friendship Tina had made the discovery that her independence had not been diminished, rather it had been strengthened. Friendship was nothing to be feared. It did not negate one's independence, just as solitude did not guarantee security.

Mulling over these thoughts, Tina realized that she had learned something even more important about herself, and that was that she had been deceiving herself about the quality of life at Cockleshell Manse. In truth, it was not as full as it might be (nor as full as she had convinced herself it was), and the children — just as much as she did — needed a wider circle of acquaintances. They needed Mr. Cadwallader and the countess and, she added with a reluctance that was almost second nature, they needed the earl.

Then and there Tina made a promise to stop deceiving herself, and the first order of business was to admit that she was not satisfied with two friends. Verily, there was one more friendship she desired: Duncan Ramsey's. Indeed, she desired it above all else. And that night, her last thought when her head touched the pillow was one of hope. Soon, very soon, she hoped she would be lucky enough to call Duncan Ramsey friend.

"How's your sister faring, Ned?" Ramsey asked as he cut the deck of cards. It was Tuesday again and the game was faro.

"Fit as a fiddle. In fact, never seen her in such a social whirl. Gel's been riding through Hyde Park every morning, rain or shine."

"That's odd," remarked Ramsey, who had not, despite several perfunctory attempts, seen his fiancée in more than a sennight's time. "She cried off the Haverly rout last evening. Claims to have caught a chill of some sort."

Lord Tweeddale emitted something that sounded like "Hmmpf," studied his cards, then remarked, "Wouldn't surprise me, not the way she's been roaming the streets with her maid. You'd almost think she was looking for something. One moment retiring as a church mouse and the next she's got her nose into everything. Never did understand her though." He thought of the smart carriage with matched dappled grays and a driver she had leased and shuddered at the prospect of more bills generated by this curiously changed sibling. Over the past forty-eight hours, his ear had been assailed ad nauseam with tales of her untoward behavior. First, it had been the Earl of Malmesbury, who had sworn upon the soul of his dear departed mother that he had seen Miss Penelope lurking about the entrance to White's. Further, he attested to having overheard the young lady offer the doorkeep a bribe in exchange for the names of any club members who were twins. And Malmesbury was not the only one to have witnessed such peculiar goings-on. The Countess Lieven had called upon Lord Tweeddale to report that his sister had engaged a pair of dandies on their strut in conversation. With a certain tension about his eyes that denoted encroaching panic, his lordship concluded, "High time to be setting a date for the wedding, Ramsey. Gel like Penelope can't wait forever."

"You're right. I'll call in a day or two."

"How about first thing in the morning," he suggested. The sooner the date was set the better, for Lord Tweeddale was not certain how his friend would react if he heard of his sister's recent activities. Although Ramsey's reputation was nothing to brag about, a man expected more of his wife than he did of himself. If Penelope kept this up, it would not be long before her name appeared in the betting book at White's. "Yes, first thing in the morning. Penelope rises with the birds and she'll be thrilled to see you. Drop by and join us for breakfast. Our cook does remarkable grilled kidneys. Afterwards you and I can make a morning of it at Manton's."

"Have a previous engagement," Ramsey equivocated. While logic argued there was no reason why marriage should interfere with his visits to Cockleshell Manse, the prospect of setting his wedding date threatened the fragile bond growing between himself and Lady Christina, and he did not wish to set the date. At least not until he had resolved her problems with the Council.

"A previous engagement? Break it." This was not an order, but rather an entreaty.

"I'll try," Ramsey replied, uncomfortable with having told a falsehood in the first place. It was not like him to behave in such a spineless fashion.

"It's that cousin of yours running you in pretty circles, I wager," the Viscount Durham, who had been paying closer attention to his cards than to the conversation, spoke up for the first time. "Unattached female relatives always entail a string of troubles."

"What's the old gel like by the by?" his lordship drawled, opening his snuffbox with the flick of a thumbnail.

"Oh, she's much as we imagined," Ramsey said, affecting a blasé manner. He was not about to tell Ned she was young and beautiful and rich, for to do so would condemn Lady Christina to a host of unwanted attention from that quarter. As fond as he was of his old friend there was no denying that Lady Christina was too fine a lady for so scapegrace a fellow as Ned Latham. Egad, even Horace Cadwallader would make a better match. Glancing about the table, it was evident that both gentlemen were waiting to hear more. Hoping to squelch their curiosity, he concluded, "She's the independent sort. Settled in her ways. Nothing to talk about, I assure you."

"Think she and my sister would get along?"

"In fact, I do." A smile touched Ramsey's mouth as he imagined how Lady Christina would take the retiring Penelope under her wing.

His lordship breathed a sigh of relief. A spinster was sure to put a damper on Penelope's recent escapades. "Excellent. So you'll set the date."

"Yes," he replied, uncertain why it was that the notion of marriage to Ned's sister — so recently a superb and sensible course of action — of a sudden made him uncomfortable in the extreme.

On the twenty-third of April, Baby was christened Diana Hunter Braughton, and after the ceremony, the children, Lady Christina, the earl, and Mr. Cadwallader, who had quickly become a special friend of the boys, returned to Cockleshell Manse for a celebration al fresco.

Winter was loosening its hold upon the metropolis. The temperature this afternoon was unseasonably warm, the sky was a vast ocean of the deepest blue, and beneath it, the gardens of Cockleshell Manse were bursting with the first colors of spring. In the flowerbeds pink tulips waved their heads above a blanket of miniature crocus and hyacinths in various shades of lavender and plum. Rows of jonquils marched along the path to the canal, and pink and white dogwood blossoms reached to the cloudless sky.

In the rose arbor, buds were forming upon the bushes. There, Cook had set out a cold collation of roasted hens, sliced ham, biscuits, pickled eggs, and an endless choice of puddings and tarts, and oversized cushions covered in Indian madras were situated on the ground for the comfort of the picnickers. The guest of honor was asleep in her basket, and Molly was curled up on a cushion beside her. Lady Christina and Duncan Ramsey were strolling toward the summerhouse, and on the lawn woolly sheep and their newborn lambs trotted about the children and Mr. Cadwallader.

Upon reaching the summerhouse, Tina and the earl looked back to view the scene. Mr. Cadwallader was wearing a crown of twigs upon his head, the girls were busily setting pickled eggs in a circle about him, and the boys were running in circles, all the while chanting something about not wanting to hurt frogs and trying to turn hearts.

Ramsey schooled his features to disguise his annoyance at this mirthful sight. Although he knew that neither he nor Horace Cadwallader entertained romantic ambitions toward Lady Christina, the earl did not want anyone other than himself to get close to her family, he did not want anyone else to be in a position to solve the lady's dilemma with the Council. It was important to Ramsey that that honor be exclusively his, and he knew a prickle of jealousy that the hospitality of Cockleshell Manse extended to Horace Cadwallader. But what he said aloud divulged none of these sentiments.

"As fond as I am of your children, Lady Christina, I suppose I should be grateful that it's Mr. Cadwallader and not I who is the center of their fantasy at this moment. What do you suppose they're playing at this time? King Arthur and Knights of the Round Table or Romans and Barbarians at Hadrian's Wall?"

"Neither." A modish satin bonnet framed her pretty face, a touch of pink gently tinted her cheeks, and there was an impish twinkle in her glorious eyes. "I don't think it's a game at all. I think it's a curse."

"A what?"

Tina was hard put to repress a giggle at the earl's obvious surprise. "I think the eggs are part of a magical spell as is the crown which identifies Mr. Cadwallader as the focus of the spell. My guess is that the children aren't aware of what they're about, and that it was Cook who, for some unknown purpose of her own, set them about it." In a dramatic aside, she added, "There's no telling what she may have put in his nuncheon."

"Your Cook is a dangerous woman."

"You don't believe in that sort of thing, do you?" Tina puzzled if this was another side of the earl she did not know.

"No, I don't, but, that doesn't diminish a

cause for reasonable alarm. Heaven knows she might give him a dreadful stomach disorder or a raging headache, if she tampers with his meal."

At the thought of the hapless Mr. Cadwallader falling prey to one of Cook's foul infusions, Tina attempted to stifle another bout of giggles, but catching sight of the earl's amusement she failed. The mood was infectious, causing Ramsey to toss back his head and emit a wicked bark of laughter, whereupon her eyes met his and they both collapsed into peals of merriment. Tears of hilarity welled in his eyes as he sputtered something about the hazards of toad tea, and Tina knew an incredible burst of exhilaration at sharing something so simple as this moment of frivolity with Duncan Ramsey.

At last, their laughter abated, and she watched as he folded his arms across his chest and leaned against the wall of the summerhouse to more fully study her.

"Why do you supposed she's casting spells on poor Mr. Cadwallader?" he wondered aloud.

"Probably the flowers."

"Ah yes, I understand." He pushed away from the wall and offered his arm to escort her up the stairs to the veranda that overlooked the canal.

Halfway up the steps, Tina's footing slipped. Quickly, Duncan Ramsey took her left hand in his, and using his other hand, he gripped her elbow to steady her balance. When they reached the top, he led her to an iron bench that afforded a view of the canal, let go of her elbow, and dusted the bench before they sat down. A pair of swans glided past on the smooth waters of the canal, in the eaves of the summerhouse a mother wren fed her noisy young, and the bleeting of lambs and singsong voices of children at play drifted on the gentle breeze. Several minutes elapsed, and the earl was still holding Tina's left hand.

Confused, she looked up at his face and saw a light burning in those blue eyes that made her tremble. "You're holding my hand very tightly, my lord," she said on a breathless whisper.

He did not speak right away. "I wanted to thank you for letting me be here today," he drawled in a low silky voice that was disturbingly intimate. Then instead of letting go of her hand, he peeled back the lace glove and kissed her wrist slightly.

Tina's skin tingled, and the natural light pink upon her cheeks heightened to a fiery shade of rose. She swallowed in a suddenly dry throat before she could reply. "It would not have been right otherwise."

Abruptly, she turned away from his close regard, trembling with the unexpected intensity of emotion. Yes, this day would not have been right without his presence, and it was an amazing development to consider. The earl was becoming a part of her life, yet it was not the dire event she had feared it might be. Quite the opposite, he was breaking down the walls of her solitude without threatening her heart or her independence.

As the date of the Countess of Brierly's fete drew nearer, Tina surprised herself by falling into preparations for the evening with great enthusiasm. A new gown was ordered from Madame Guernon, and the exorbitant services of one Monsieur Rossi were engaged, but upon viewing his prospective client the flamboyant coiffeur declared Lady Christina *magnifique*. To alter perfection would be worse than gilding a lily, he asserted; no crimping, cutting, or coloring was necessary.

It was natural that these events would recall memories of a time gone by, reviving the light-headed anticipation she had known in her first Season. It was almost as if time had reversed itself, so clear and identical were those feelings that she had imagined lost to her forever. How readily those secret yearnings to waltz with a dark and handsome stranger resurfaced, how sweet was the dream of being held in a strong pair of arms and spinning about a glittering ballroom. Even the vision of the gentleman, dashing and gallant and dressed in a scarlet uniform, was as vivid as it had been five years before, but there was one crucial difference between now and then.

The past had taught Tina how foolish it was to expect romantic miracles in a single night of dancing beneath candlelight. Love was not waiting for her. There was no handsome hero who would declare his undying devotion. Love at first sight did not exist. Although she accepted this sobering truth and reminded herself of it frequently, she could not help being swept away in a flood of girlish expectation. Who would be there? Would she dance? Would she flirt? Would her gown be too fancy or too plain? While Tina did not wish to draw excessive notice to herself, she could not deny the twinge of female vanity that dictated she must appear her best. It was going to be an important night: its outcome would decide if Tina would modestly reenter Society, or continue her retiring manner of living.

So it was with high spirits that Tina awoke the morning of the Countess of Brierly's party. She had not received a single nasty missive from the Council in more than two weeks, and as for Duncan Ramsey, he no longer filled her with trepidation. Her stomach did not drop when he appeared in the schoolroom door or when she heard his voice echoing through the great hall. Truth to tell, she welcomed his visits, and on more than one occasion, she had had to control the impulse to dash down the drive with the children to greet him.

Verily, the future was looking better with each sunrise. It was going to be a splendid day and an equally splendid evening.

Seven

All was not, however, looking so rosy for the Honorable Penelope Latham on that same fine April morning.

The delicate Swiss timepiece on the mantel had not yet struck nine when Penelope entered the dining room of her brother's town house on Hay's Mews to meet a most unusual sight. There was Ned, bright-eyed and bold as brass, partaking of a hearty meal. Her astonishment at seeing her errant elder sibling up and about before noon was further compounded by the presence of the Earl of Croick. Seated at the place opposite the one set for herself, Ramsey was enjoying a massive plate of grilled kidneys and thin sliced toast.

Bidding them a reserved good morning, Penelope took her seat, eyes downcast and her heart racing in apprehension. Glancing up from beneath pale lashes, she studied the earl. He had never seemed so big and dark and powerful as he did at that moment, and Penelope cringed.

149

What was he doing here? she wondered as panic seeped through every pore in her slender frame. *Oh, mercy me, something was afoot, for there could be no other reason for that smug expression upon Ned's face.* Ned *never* budged from beneath his counterpane before noon unless it was to evade the duns or exact payment for a gambling debt from souls less fortunate than him. Since no one was knocking loudly upon the front door, nor was Ned examining the contents of a money bag or gloating over a promissory note, she feared his early appearance this day had something to do with the earl and whatever it was it probably included her as well. Oh, why wouldn't someone speak? Why wouldn't Ned get it over with before she expired on the spot?

As if hearing his sister's silent plea, Lord Tweeddale folded his linen napkin and placed it on the table in a flourishing motion that denoted great purpose. "Ramsey was just saying the third week of June is always a good date for a wedding, weren't you, Ramsey?"

The earl nodded a rather noncommittal response, and had it not been for her own distress, mayhap Penelope would have been aware of the gentleman's reluctance. The poor girl, however, could think of little else than the fact that she had not yet located the fair-haired twins of whom Madame Zaborini had foretold, and her appetite soured as the meaning of this gathering became evident. Ned intended to see her wed before the Season was ended. Time to search for Madame Zaborini's gentleman would shortly end. Her fate, it appeared, was to be a dismal one after all. There was to be no love match with a handsome blond gentleman, instead she was destined for a suitable alliance in which form dictated she be scrupulously polite while enduring an endless series of winters at some gray Highland fortress.

The only person at the mahogany table to demonstrate the slightest interest in the topic of conversation was Lord Tweeddale. In a tenor of high excitement, he rattled on, "It's settled then. Third week of June. As Penelope's guardian I'll see to the arrangements. Nothing for either of you to worry about. Assume you'd both like it done up like the best of 'em. St. George's and all that."

Neither Ramsey nor Penelope acknowledged this. Each was preoccupied with affairs wholly unrelated to their impending nuptials.

The earl's thoughts were focused upon Lady Christina and her problems with the Council. To Ramsey's thinking, Lady Christina's dilemma was far more important than this call upon Miss Penelope, and in point of fact, he had put off this meeting until he had completed a round of consultations with a team of solicitors to formulate a course of action to thwart the Council. Part and parcel of their plan was his frequent presence at Cockleshell Manse (another reason why it had taken almost a fortnight to accept Ned's breakfast invitation). The solicitors agreed that an oft visible male relative was one way to blunt the Council's accusations whatever they might be. Hence, he had spent the better part of the past two weeks at Cockleshell Manse. Additionally, the legal gentlemen were pouring over ancient tomes; methodically, they researched the statutes governing distaff inheritance, plus those ordinances pertaining to adoption, poor laws and privacy, and a host of medieval common law dealing with tenure and property rights. If no precedent could be found to stand on Lady Christina's side, mayhap there was cause for counteraction against the Council. Ramsey had been assured that as surely as the Council could find a loophole in the law that might be used against Lady Christina, so, too, could his solicitors find one that favored the lady.

The whole of this activity was proceeding unbeknownst to Lady Christina. The reason for the earl's secrecy was his fear that if he told her of his intentions, she might, at best, refuse his help, or, at worst, demand that he cease. Although Ramsey could not quite pin it down, he sensed a lingering reservation on her part whenever he came to call, and he did not wish to do anything that might disturb her. Each day, he visited the Manse, and he was pleased that as time passed Lady Christina had begun to join in his outings with the children; he was pleased, too, that her invitations to dine with her and the children were more frequent. Ramsey was certain that she would soon accept him as readily as did the children, then he would tell her of his progress with the solicitors, and he would be able to repay the awful debt he owed her.

While Ramsey considered these weighty matters Penelope was plotting her imminent flight from Hay's Mews. The sole recourse left to her, she had decided the instant Ned had uttered the words *wedding* and *June,* was to run away from home, and no sooner had the gentlemen taken themselves off to Manton's than she dashed upstairs in search of her abigail.

"You must pack a bag for me, Katie. And with haste, for I must be off within the hour," she announced with a light in her eyes that denotes a swiftly hatched scheme.

"A journey, Miss Penelope?" Bewildered, Katie Biggs paused in the task of fetching gloves and stockings to match the poppy pink walking dress she had withdrawn from the wardrobe for her mistress. Of late, it was Penelope's habit to change her clothes after breakfast and go for a nice long walk in St. James's.

"Yes, a trip. I've received a note from the curate in Aylesbury." She flicked a wrist toward the writing table by the window as if to validate the existence of such a letter. "His news is grave. Mrs. Braithwaite, my former governess, has become ill . . . so ill, she's unable to write herself . . . and she's failing rapidly."

"That's terrible news, miss. Plum terrible it is," Katie said, giving a woeful shake of her head. She knew how fond Miss Penelope was of Mrs. Braithwaite. Why, it was almost as terrible a thing as her own mum taking ill.

"Anyway, I must go to her," Penelope explained, knowing that it would be impossible to take Katie into her confidence. The maid was too easily harassed by her brother and would do anything to prevent her employer from engaging in a fit of temper. What the girl failed to comprehend was that Ned seldom remained in a rage for long; no sooner had he vented his spleen than the cause was quite forgotten, more often than not overshadowed by pecuniary worries. All in all it seemed best to leave Katie Biggs in the dark as to her true intentions. One round oath from Ned and the girl was bound to tell him everything she knew, and as much as Penelope disliked weaving a tale concerning so godly a lady as Mrs. Braithwaite it seemed the most plausible explanation to be accepted by Katie and Ned. "You do understand the urgency of my departure, don't you?"

"Oh yes, Miss Penelope, indeed, I do, and it's a kind thing you're doing leaving London just to visit her. Why, seeing you is bound to do Mrs. Braithwaite a world of good, I imagine."

"Those were my exact thoughts."

"Will Lord Tweeddale be going with you, miss?"

"No, I shall travel alone."

"Alone? Oh, miss, even for Mrs. Braithwaite, I don't think your brother will approve. Won't you be wanting me to go with you?"

Penelope experienced a pang of vexation. Surely, her maid was not going to prevent her from doing as she wished. The lie deepened. "No, I shan't need you. Oh, it's not that I don't want you, Katie," she added in a gentler tone, observing the hurt upon the maid's face. "But the curate's second cousin, a widow, is leaving Town this very morning and I shall travel in her company."

The mention of a widowed relative of a man of the cloth mollified Katie. She reached into the depths of the wardrobe to pull out a portmanteau. "Shall I fetch your trunks from the attic, miss?"

"A single bag will suffice. If I find my stay will be longer than expected, you can forward a trunk or two. And don't put away the poppy pink walking dress, Katie. I shall wear it after all. Pink quite suits my mood," she added, determined to look her best when she ventured forth. The notion of leaving home was most liberating. Verily, Penelope considered it a great adventure much like the one embarked upon by Miss Comfortina Monkton in the musical drama, *Travels of a Country Miss or Love Finds the Squire's Daughter*. It was most fortifying to recall how Miss Monkton had escaped the evil grasp of her scheming stepfather to find true love. Perhaps, as had the stage heroine, this was the day Penelope would encounter her beloved. If so, she intended to meet him in poppy pink.

A pale rose twilight bathed Regent's Park as Penelope dawdled her way along the path, swinging her reticule by its ribbons. Having, it seemed, trekked from one end of London to the other, her feet were beginning to ache, and that was only one of many signs that her day had not developed quite as she had expected.

The first thing she had done upon leaving the town house was head for Smithfield Market, where she intended to consult Madame Zaborini, but the gypsy caravan was gone and no one knew where. That had been Penelope's first setback, for she had been counting on Madame Zaborini to advise her whether she ought to apply for a position as a governess or join an acting troupe. Neither prospect appealed to Penelope, a fact that was of little relevance at this juncture, for the sun was setting and Penelope was neither ensconced in a comfortable nursery enjoying a warm meal with her charges, nor was she bound for a provincial theater to play the leading female role in one of Mr. Shakespeare's romantic tragedies. Instead she was cold, her stomach was grumbling in most unladylike fashion, and she was beginning to experience a tiny seed of apprehension regarding her precipitous departure from Hay's Mews.

Without warning two men crashed out of the bushes behind her. They were large men, garbed in rough clothes, their persons were grimy as chimney sweeps, and their dark expressions were determined and threatening. Despite her woeful inexperience, Penelope knew right away they were footpads. With a piercing shriek, she dropped the portmanteau and turned to flee, but a hairy unwashed arm blocked her way.

" 'And over yer goods or Oi'll give ye a pop on yer noggin, right and good." A stout man with stringy black hair reached for her reticule.

"No, that's quite impossible, sir," Penelope declared with a stamp of her foot, clutching the brocade bag to her bosom. The reticule contained her mother's pearl and diamond ear bobs not to mention every shilling she had managed to save from her meager allowance. Nothing would force her to part with it. If today had been a disaster, tomorrow would be a catastrophe, if she found herself penniless.

The stout man loomed over Penelope. "And what 'ave we 'ere?" This time he reached for a ringlet hanging from beneath her poppy pink bonnet.

A very ripe odor assailed Penelope, and she gagged.

The second man, who had been inspecting the contents of the portmanteau, straightened up to take a closer look at Penelope. "A real hoity-toity lady, by the looks of 'er," he remarked with a grin that revealed a row of discolored teeth, prompting her hysterical mind to dub him Yellow Tooth. "Fact is, we might ov found ourselves somethin' more valuable."

Both men pressed closer to Penelope, and the stench, somewhat akin to rotting codfish, was overwhelming. In vain, she averted her face, then closed and opened her eyes as if doing so might cause the men to disappear. But this was no nightmare and there would be no waking beneath sweet-smelling sheets in her cozy bedroom on Hay's Mews.

"Just what Oi was thinkin'," agreed the stout man, his unwashed hand still touching her hair, his putrid breath touching her neck.

The meaning of their words struck a chord of terror in Penelope's heart. Tears began to flow down her cheeks, and she trembled violently when that first man dropped her ringlet to enable his hand to slide down her shoulder and linger at the bodice of her walking dress.

Scream, Penelope, scream! an inner voice instructed, but her earlier bravado was lost. It was one thing to have your mama's jewels in jeopardy. One's person was another matter altogether, and so great was her mounting fear that a squeaky "Stop" was the full extent of any sound she could make.

"Relax, dearie. All we wants is a little bit of fun. And Jocko and Oi knows lots of ways to have fun. Don't we, Jocko?" Yellow Tooth laughed as he tugged at her bonnet strings.

"Stop," she managed in a somewhat louder voice.

Yellow Tooth took off her bonnet and it fell to the ground as he began to stroke her hair.

"No." She shook her head in fervent denial, ringlets coming undone to cascade down her back as she stepped away only to feel arms go about her waist in a viselike grip.

Now, Penelope, now. Don't be a ninny. You've got to scream before it's too late.

Taking a deep breath, she managed a louder and clearer "No." Then she repeated it several times until it became one endless high-pitched scream.

"Noooooooooo!" echoed through the darkening park. It was without doubt the cry of a lady in distress.

Just as suddenly as the thieves had emerged from the brush, three boys dropped from an overhanging branch.

Penelope moaned. *Not more footpads.* Oh, she was doomed. The gypsy woman had been quite off the mark: her destiny was to be unspeakable disgrace and then death in Regent's Park, not love with a handsome gentleman. Once more, Penelope closed her eyes, wishing most fervently that the end would come as speedily as possible.

"Grab that stick, Finny. Hit the fat one!"

The lad's words compelled Penelope to

160

open her eyes and take a second look at the boys. One was kicking her assailants about the shins, another was fetching a stick, and the tallest lad was taunting the thieves with the most astounding barrage of street cant. Although they were behaving no better than urchins their kerseymere pantaloons and visored jockey caps were the sort worn by children of Quality.

"Thief!" screamed the lad who was doing the kicking.

"Help! Anybody, help!" joined in the boy with the stick as he continued to thrash at Yellow Tooth.

As the two largest boys began pummeling the men the smallest lad ceased his kicking to yank Penelope to safety behind the nearest hedge. During the ensuing fracas the boys, including the one in the undergrowth with Penelope, maintained such a ruckus that it was only a matter of time before someone else was bound to hear their cries and arrive on the scene. Hence it was the noise more than anything — though one of the boys had bloodied the stout man's nose — that forced the thieves to abandon their felonious purpose and bolt.

Several moments elapsed as the boys and Penelope waited in silence to be certain the men were gone. At length, Penelope stepped from behind the hedgerow. "How lucky I am that you came along when you did," she said between wet sniffles as she gave each of her rescuers an impulsive hug. "Oh, thank you. What brave lads you are. Oh, thank you ever so much."

"You're welcome, miss," replied the tallest boy, who appeared to be in charge. "Are you all right? They didn't harm you, did they?"

"No, they didn't hurt me. I — I think I'm fine." Penelope reached up to straighten her hair, but one touch told her it was beyond repair. "Oh, my, where is my hat? I must find my hat," she mumbled in singularly feminine distress. At the sight of the poppy pink bonnet lying upon the ground crushed and imprinted with the muddy silhouette of a boot the sting of renewed tears prickled her nose. Giving a sniffle, she picked up the miserable piece of apparel. "Oh, my poor dear hat. My poor dear hat. My goodness, do I look as awful as this?"

"Oh no, miss," reassured the tallest boy as he gathered up the scattered contents of the portmanteau. He gave her a reassuring grin. "But what are you doing alone in the park at this time of the day? Did your maid run off when the robbers appeared?"

"I — " She stopped herself before blurting out that she was running away from her brother.

"You were lost I bet," put in the lad who had wielded the stick.

"Why, yes. I was lost." At once, Penelope's fertile imagination began to create a fiction worthy of the situation. "I just arrived in the Metropolis this afternoon, you see, and have yet to learn my way around."

"But where were you going?"

"To an employment agency. I intend to become a governess."

"It's too late for that tonight." The tallest boy closed the portmanteau and set it on the ground beside Penelope. "Why don't you come home with us?"

"I couldn't impose," was her instant rejoinder. What if their parents recognized her? Their sire or an elder brother could be a member of Ned's club. Then what would she do? She could not risk being returned to her brother. "It wouldn't be proper. I don't even know your names."

"I'm Joshua, this is Finny, that's Francis, and it wouldn't be any imposition. Not at all. Tina Mum would be more than happy to let you stay the night at Cockleshell Manse. And as for it not being proper, well, it would be a sight more proper to take you home with us than to leave you to wander about the park alone."

Having never heard of Cockleshell Manse,

Penelope decided that it would be quite safe to go home with the boys. To the best of her knowledge no one of the beau monde resided in a residence of that name. She would be foolish not to accept their invitation, for the sky had turned quite black, and the boy was right — she could not continue to wander through the park.

"I should appreciate that very much. Tomorrow will be soon enough to find employment."

Francis slipped his hand in hers and grinned up at her. "What's *your* name, miss?"

"Pen — Jane Penny," she corrected, having decided she must not use her own name.

"Well, come along then, Miss Penny." Joshua picked up the portmanteau. "Cook hates to serve a cold duck and we're already late enough. You do like roast duck, don't you?"

"Excepting cinnamon buns there's nothing I like better," she replied, her stomach echoing its own response so loudly that the boys heard, and the quartet of new friends laughed as they headed toward Cockleshell Manse.

"Ye'll be marking my words, ye'll be. The girl ain't no miss up from the country to become a governess."

"And how would you know, Cook?" Tina,

164

dressed in her new dancing frock from Madame Guernon, stood before the hooded library hearth. Although Miss Penny presented a dilemma, she was pleased for the distraction; the boys' arrival home with the disheveled young woman had helped to diminish a measure of her queasiness about the countess's gathering. It was always easiest to dismiss one's own worries, she had long ago discovered, if there was someone else over whom she might fret. In the past, the children had provided such distraction; this evening, Miss Jane Penny was an ideal diversion.

"It's too young, too pretty, and too well dressed, she be," came the old woman's decisive response as she lit the last of the fresh tapers in the wall sconces. Welcoming golden light suffused the library as she glanced about her, making certain that all was in order. A fresh arrangement of flowers from the conservatory graced the pianoforte, the children's toys had been put away, and the furniture had been polished to a high gleam. One of the Countess of Brierly's brothers was coming to escort Tina to the party, and Cook was anxious that everything about this evening be perfect. It would not do for Cockleshell Manse to be any less shining than its mistress, and satisfied that Mr. O'Kieffe would be suitably impressed with Lady Christina's establishment, she returned to the subject at hand. "And I'll be wagering 'tis a name other than Jane the young miss was given before the eyes of God."

"I suppose you're right," said Tina after a moment of reflection. "But that doesn't mean we can't let her stay the night. Or even a few days."

"Hmmpf." If Lady Tina was determined to give the girl shelter, then nothing she said on the matter would sway her kindhearted mistress.

The library door opened to reveal Penelope on the threshold. Her pale brown hair had been combed out and tied back with a velvet ribband, and she had changed from her soiled walking outfit to a cambric gown that Tina had outgrown.

"You wished to see me, my lady?" Penelope inquired, unable to disguise her apprehension. Although the lady appeared kindhearted, the intimidating scowl upon the older woman's face was etched with distrust, and Penelope could not suppress the feeling that she was about to face an inquisition. The courage she had displayed since her encounter with Madame Zaborini was gone. She had left home and faced footpads, yet the sight of this formidable servant reduced Penelope to her meeker former self.

"Yes, I did. Please, come in." Sitting upon the scrolled sofa, Tina motioned for the girl to take the seat beside her. "You're feeling better?"

Bestowing a shy smile upon Tina, Penelope replied, "Much better." Sitting down, she peered over her shoulder at Cook and managed a weak, "The duck was delicious, ma'am."

"And how do you like your room?" Tina asked, raising her voice several decibels in an effort to cover the disapproving grumble that emanated from Cook.

"The room is most pretty and comfortable. Thank you. I don't know how I shall ever be able to repay your kindness."

From the corner of her eye, Tina saw Cook give a sharp nod as if to say, *Here's yer chance to find out what scandal broth this troublesome miss is evading.*

"As a matter of fact there is one way you can repay me."

Penelope's smile brightened. In the past hour, she had formulated a neat fantasy that solved all of her problems and now it was bound to become reality; the girl was certain that Lady Christina was about to offer her a position as governess. "I should be happy to do whatever you like."

"You can repay me by telling me the truth

about who you are and what you were doing in the park."

The smile faded. Penelope averted her glance to stare at her hands. In a voice barely above a whisper, she asked, "Is it so obvious?"

"I'm afraid it is."

"And if I tell you the whole of it, what then?"

"We shall see. I cannot say until I know the truth." Tina gave the girl a reassuring pat upon the arm. "I'm neither unfair nor cruel, and I promise to consider your story with an open mind."

Ever so slowly, Penelope raised her head, and after an indecisive moment of pouting she began, "You see, it all has to do with my brother Ned and the gypsy. I would never dare to disobey Ned, if it weren't for Madame Zaborini. Oh, it's not that I'm blaming her, but don't you see I couldn't marry the gentleman Ned had selected for me, not after the tea leaves told me there was someone else."

Not knowing how to respond to this unexpected revelation, Tina turned toward Cook to be further confounded by the discovery that the girl's bizarre explanation had found an ally in the West Country woman. The blatant censure had vanished from Cook's lined countenance to be replaced by an expression of the most sympathetic understanding.

"And a wise girl yer being not to defy the path of destiny."

"Gypsies and destiny! I've never heard such arrant nonsense." It was Tina's turn to frown at the girl. "What of the brother you mention? Certainly, he must be worried about you."

"Oh no, my lady. Ned believes I've gone to visit my former governess."

Tina's frown deepened. "Then you're asking me to support you in a lie. You must, at least, tell me your name."

The girl paled. "Oh no, my lady, please forgive me, but I can't do that. There's *nothing* that could force me to divulge the whole truth. *Nothing*." She sat taller, tilted her pointed chin higher, and concluded with a watery sniffle, "And if you wish to turn me out, then so be it."

"Don't ye be worrying none, Miss Penny. There'll be no turning ye out this eve. Lady Christina would never do such a thing. Ye'll be staying with us and we'll be making certain ye find the gentleman of yer destiny."

The sight of tears brimming in the girl's eyes was Tina's undoing. She did not like to be the cause of anyone's distress. "Although I would be happiest if you could trust me, Cook is quite right. You may remain at Cockleshell

Manse. I must add, however, that if I hear of any brothers making queries as to the whereabouts of a young lady such as yourself, I shall be forced to tell the truth."

"I understand, and I could not hope for more, my lady." The tears in her eyes melted instantly.

Footsteps echoed from the corridor drawing all three women's attention to the doorway.

First, Hobbins appeared. "Mr. Michael O'Kieffe."

A dashing gentleman strode into the library. Mr. Michael O'Kieffe, youngest of the infamous O'Kieffe brothers, whose headlong pursuit of pleasure had on more than one occasion shocked even the most jaded rakehell, had hair the color of ripe wheat with a slight natural curl that contrasted with his formal black attire. He was the sort of gentleman schoolgirls dreamed of kissing, and he fit Penelope's notion of masculine perfection to a tee.

"Good evening, Mr. O'Kieffe," said Tina, gathering up her beaded reticule from the nearby table.

"Lady Christina, 'tis a pleasure to meet you." A hint of his father's Celtic homeland peppered his greeting as he bowed before her. His sister had been right. Lady Christina was a stunner, and Mina would have no trouble finding her a husband. But it was the younger girl on the settee that attracted his notice. A bit on the thin side with a totally unremarkable mouth and rather mousy hair, she was not as pretty as most of the ladies of his acquaintance, but it was the vulnerable tilt of her head, the soft feminine lines of her nervous little hands, and the almost waiflike expression in her eyes that compelled him to take a second look at her. Damned, if there weren't tears shimmering at the end of her eyelashes, and his heart swelled with protective instinct.

"This is our guest, Miss Penny," said Tina, having noticed the direction of his regard.

"Miss Penny." He executed a chivalrous bow, a pair of the greenest eyes in a tanned face gazing down at her warmly.

"How do you do," whispered Penelope, much struck by the handsome Irishman.

He turned to Lady Christina. "I'm sure had my sister known that you had a houseguest she would have sent another invitation."

"Oh no, I couldn't," was Penelope's immediate response. Engulfed by the blush of all time, she added, "I've just arrived, you see, and my journey was most fatiguing."

"I quite understand." He smiled at her, the sort of smile that did peculiar things to a lady's head. "Perhaps I may call upon you at another time, Miss Penny. If Lady Christina would allow, I would be honored to show you some of the attractions in our fair Metropolis."

As much as Penelope would love spending time with Mr. O'Kieffe, she could ill afford any distractions from her purpose, nor could she risk doing anything that might reveal her hiding place. She must locate the fair-haired twins before Ned found her and forced her to marry the earl. Penelope cast a desperate glance at Lady Christina.

"That is a gracious invitation, Mr. O'Kieffe, but we shall have to wait and see how Miss Penny adjusts before she can embark on any engagements."

"I see." Truth to tell, he found Lady Christina's explanation most evasive. He did not understand in the least, and loathing rejection, his interest in Miss Penny altered from a passing fancy to one of determination. This was not the last time he intended to call upon Cockleshell Manse. "Shall we go, Lady Christina? My coachman is waiting."

Tina stood and accepted Mr. O'Kieffe's arm.

"Good evening, Miss Penny," he said and was rewarded by an incontestable note of disappointment in the young lady's timorous farewell.

As Mr. O'Kieffe escorted Lady Christina from the library he allowed his flashing green eyes a final backward glance to dwell appreciatively on the slender and mysterious girl who remained behind at Cockleshell Manse.

Eight

An excessive number of vehicles clogged the streets leading into Berkeley Square, and leaning forward for a better view, Tina was dismayed to discover they were all headed toward the same location, the imposing Palladian-fronted mansion at Number 5. At the prospect of mingling with so many strangers Tina's misgivings that had ebbed upon the arrival of Miss Penny returned.

"I thought this was to be a family gathering," she said to Mr. O'Kieffe, hoping she did not sound like a complete wet goose.

"Don't doubt it started out that way, but my sister's notion of a modest little patty has never been modest. Mina loves any excuse to entertain, and since marrying Cavendish she's never done anything on a small scale, nor has her husband's *grandmère*, the dowager countess. I'd wager the pair of them have devoted the better part of the past sennight to menus and decor. Wait 'til you see Cavendish House. Never looks so splendid as when Mina has it done up for a party. Flowers everywhere. You'll feel like you're in an orchard in Kent."

These innocent words exacerbated Tina's apprehension. She dropped a glance at her gloved hands, clasped upon the skirt of her satin gown, and considered developing a raging headache. It would be so simple to retreat to the safety of Cockleshell Manse and forget that she had ever accepted the Countess of Brierly's invitation in the first place. In the next instant, that notion was scotched. Not only was it cowardly, but the prospect of explaining an early return to Cook was — in some ways — far more daunting than a crowd of ladies and gentlemen who might remember the young girl whose come-out Season had been a fiasco. She chose to brave the night ahead.

Owning an uncanny instinct when it came to ladies in distress, Mr. O'Kieffe sensed Tina's reserve, and as the carriage came to a halt, he exclaimed, "Oh, I say, Lady Christina, you do look grand. An honor it is to be escorting you this evening."

She managed a thin smile.

"And that, I assure you, is no blarney." He gave her a roguish wink.

"Thank you, sir." She accepted his arm to alight from the carriage and mount the marble stairs.

In the next instant, they were inside Cavendish House, and as Mr. O'Kieffe had predicted all trace of the lingering winter faded away. Artistically pruned fruit trees festooned with satin streamers graced the rotunda, and floral garlands wound up the banister of a wide circling staircase. The delicate aroma of orange blossoms mingled with the scent of gardenias and hyacinths. Candles flickered in crystal sconces, priceless jewels shimmered against provocatively displayed flesh, and everything reflected in massive gilt mirrors seemed to glitter doubly. Gentlemen chatted in small groups of two or three, and ladies in elegant gowns of satin and velvet and the thinnest muslins glided up the staircase like skaters on a pond. But Tina did not notice any of this as a footman took her velvet-lined cloak.

It had been a long time since she had been in the same room with so many people. People with whom she was expected to converse in a witty and engaging style. But what was she to say? She knew nothing of the latest political gossip, nor the most popular theatrical at Drury Lane. Even the language of the beau monde had become alien to her ear; she scarcely knew a tulip from a dandy, nor a fribble from a fop. Her experience, limited to the children and Cockleshell Manse, was of no use in this situation. Even the most guarded reference to Francis's guinea pig or Black Jack would be suicidal, and a discourse upon one of Cook's infusions or the merits of hand-me-downs in a growing family would be equally ill-advised.

There was a fleeting quiver she could not control in her chin. This was all a mistake. A terrible, foolish mistake, cried an inner voice. What had she been thinking to accept the countess's invitation? She should have stayed home and invited Duncan Ramsey to see the children's production of *Cinderella*.

"Come, Lady Christina, I believe my sister is receiving on the second floor."

It was too late for regrets. There could be no turning back, so with her head held high and one arm looped through Mr. O'Kieffe's, Tina gazed straight ahead as they began their way toward the staircase. Unexpectedly, a snippet of conversation caught her ear, something about an unforeseen trip to the country, and she turned toward the familiar male voice.

There was Duncan Ramsey, sophisticated and confident, the ever present gold-tipped cane in one hand, and garbed in elegant black evening dress that looked as if it had been molded to his tall muscular frame. It was with a queer little uplifting of her heart that she welcomed the sight of him. Why, it was almost as if he had magically materialized in response to her cowardly thoughts. He was smiling at her, and in response, Tina favored Ramsey with a dazzling smile of her own.

"*You're* acquainted with the earl?" inquired Mr. O'Kieffe, who could not help wondering how a female as sheltered as Lady Christina could know a man like Ramsey.

"He's a distant cousin."

"Ah." Mr. O'Kieffe's reply suggested complete comprehension.

Ramsey had been watching Tina since she entered the rotunda. To a stranger, she might have appeared aloof, almost mysterious, but to Ramsey, who had come to know her these past weeks, it was impossible not to recognize the painstakingly held panic etched upon her delicate features.

"I say, Ramsey, are you listening to a word I've said?" asked Lord Tweeddale.

"Sorry," was the extent of his absent-minded response. Continuing to study Lady Christina, he recalled an earlier time when she had sat at the edge of gaiety. A time when she had been the object of unkind gossip and speculation; a time that had marked the end rather than the beginning of a happy future among young ladies and gentlemen of her own age and rank. And just as he accepted the blame for the resultant unhappiness, he resolved that such an outcome would never happen again, not if he could help it.

"As I was saying, it's Penelope," persisted Tweeddale. "Gone off to Aylesbury to visit her governess. Seems the old girl's taken ill."

"Sorry."

His lordship gave an irritated huff. "What *are* you staring at?" He turned and saw Lady Christina. A most common whistle escaped his lips. "I say, Ramsey, she may be a prime article, but you mustn't forget *you're* a betrothed man."

"You don't need to remind me." The earl pivoted away from his friend to cross the rotunda.

Lord Tweeddale hurried in pursuit.

Seven purposeful strides and Ramsey stood before Tina. "Good evening, my lady," he greeted her, a note of obvious pleasure in his voice as his blue eyes swept over her. She was lovely. No, lovely did not do her justice. She was brilliant in a dress of silver spider gauze over a lavender satin slip. A coronet of silk flowers that matched the deep lilac of her eyes nestled among the abundant curls drifting over one creamy shoulder.

"Good evening, my lord," she said, new-found confidence lacing her words. Smiling up at the earl, her surroundings faded away and she forgot about the room full of strangers. This was easy enough; she could talk to Duncan Ramsey, for she had been doing so with ease these past weeks. Why, she could even mention Black Jack or the hobby horse without raising an eyebrow. Her hands, clasped about the reticule, relaxed.

Mr. O'Kieffe stepped forward to deliver the requisite pleasantries. "Good evening, Ramsey."

"O'Kieffe." The earl gave a courteous nod, then promptly returned his attention to Tina. "I didn't know you planned to be here. I would have served as your escort had you asked," he said, oddly miffed that she was here with O'Kieffe, who was, in his opinion, far too spirited a companion for any well-bred lady. If she had needed an escort why hadn't she relied upon him? He was, after all, her cousin, and they had been getting along well these past days, had they not?

Before Tina could answer, Mr. O'Kieffe spoke up, "Lady Christina is a neighbor. That's why m'sister asked if I could escort her this evening."

The pleasant expression upon Ramsey's face wilted. Good Lord, was she neighbors with every unwed man in Town? First, it was a disgustingly wealthy cit, and now a scapegrace Irish buck with a reputation worse than his own. What was he to expect next? Prinny himself? he speculated, wholly oblivious of the green-eyed direction of his thoughts.

"Would you mind, sir, if I left Lady Christina in your keeping?" inquired Mr. O'Kieffe, aware of a peculiar undercurrent and eager to escape.

"That would be fine. I should be more than happy to escort my cousin upstairs." Ramsey glanced at Tina as if seeking her consent and was pleased when she did not naysay him.

"Until later then, my lady." Mr. O'Kieffe bowed, then slipped through the crowd toward the gaming tables set up in a rear saloon.

"Your cousin!" It was Tweeddale. "Egad, this ain't the independent spinster, Lady what's-her-name living among the mushrooms in Regent's Park? Thought she was a toothless ape leader," he declared with his usual insensitivity.

"Yes, this is my cousin, Lady Christina Braughton. Lady Christina, my friend, Lord Tweeddale."

"Sir," she said in a quiet voice, not knowing what to make of the outspoken Lord Tweeddale.

" 'Pon my soul, Ramsey, you're a devil to have kept so exquisite a diamond all to yourself. Take a look into those eyes. Why, they put me in mind of a sultry summer night."

Wondering whether to laugh or to thank

Lord Tweeddale, Tina cast a sideways glance at Ramsey for advice.

"He's flirting with you," quipped Ramsey.

"Flirting, you say?" A small smile quirked at the corner of her mouth. "I'm afraid I'm sadly out of practice."

"I should be happy to teach you," put forth his lordship with quick eagerness.

"Pray do not regard the gentleman, Lady Christina. A good friend, he may be, but I'd not vouch for him at a time like this."

"Daresay, Ramsey, don't go making a muddle of this for me. Thought we were in for a dull time of it tonight, but the lady puts a new face on it altogether. I've quite had my hopes up since she walked through the door."

"No doubt you did," was his cynical retort.

Ignoring Ramsey, his lordship made an elegant leg. "Might I have the honor of a dance, my lady?"

Music could be heard from the ballroom at the top of the stairs, and listening to the opening chords, Tina replied, "It is a waltz, Lord Tweeddale, and as an unmarried lady I fear I cannot accept your invitation."

"But you may accept mine."

Soft violet eyes flew wide. Questioningly, Tina regarded Ramsey, a mixture of hope and doubt revealed upon her features. A waltz with Duncan Ramsey? It did not seem possible, and at the prospect of acting out her deepest secret an involuntary fluttering in her heart belied the skepticism of her mind. Perhaps romantic dreams did come true.

"As we are related there would be nothing improper in waltzing with me," he said, but there was a gleam in his eyes that was entirely improper as he led her toward the stairs.

"You're certain it would be all right?"

"I would not lie to you." He slipped an arm about her waist and led her up the staircase toward the ballroom.

"But I haven't even said hello to our hostess yet." It was a feeble objection, for she did not demur when he discreetly placed the gold-tipped cane behind a chair and tightened his hold about her waist. A giddy sensation rushed through Tina as he held her close and spun them into the whirl of circling couples.

"The countess will understand. She would never wish to be the cause for a young lady missing the chance to waltz."

"You're quite sure of yourself. Do you know the countess that well?"

"After a manner," he murmured, executing a neat turn and thinking for the first time that his war injury was a good thing, for it allowed him to hold Lady Christina closer and tighter than was normally permissible, even during a waltz. At length, he added, "I proposed to the lady once."

"But I thought you were a confirmed bachelor. You must have been very much in love," she said, needing to know if this was true.

"Not really," he said, owning no compunction to disguise the truth. He had never revealed so much of himself to anyone, yet oddly, he saw no reason not to confide in this lady.

Tina's eyes met his, and she dared to ask, "If not for love, why did you propose?"

"Miss O'Kieffe was the first lady who understood me. As you well know, London is a superficial world in which everyone is given a label and all else derives from that initial impression. In my case, it was rake and rogue, yet she was the only one to look beyond that and consider I might be something more. It may seem strange, and I know it's rare between an unwed lady and a gentleman of shaky reputation, but we became friends, and I could not help but respect her for that."

Of a sudden, envy for the countess streaked through Tina. Ever since Diana's christening, she thought of Duncan Ramsey as a friend, and although she knew it was ridiculous, she did not like to consider any other woman claiming that same privilege. Shocked by so alien an emotion, she selected her response with care. "My grandfather once told me that short of love friendship is the greatest compliment a lady can receive from a man. The countess is a lucky lady."

"I'm pleased you think so." He spoke in a voice that was startlingly intimate.

The music ceased, and they stood still, Ramsey's hand remaining at Tina's waist while he stared down at her lumunous eyes.

"Very pleased, indeed," he whispered, his voice low and deep and soft as velvet, his piercing eyes holding hers.

Confusion surged through Tina. Something in his look brought the blood rushing to her cheeks. Her throat was dry, and she swallowed, not having the vaguest clue what she should say or do next.

A voice broke the silence. "Lady Christina, I'm so pleased you could join us." The Countess of Brierly gave Tina a kiss upon each cheek, then addressed the gentleman at her side. "Compton, let me present you to my new friend, Lady Christina Braughton. And, *Grandmère*, this is the remarkable young lady I told you about."

Compton Cavendish, the Earl of Brierly, executed a formal bow, told Tina what an honor it was to make her acquaintance, and then his grandmother, a statuesque and elegant French-woman of advanced years, burst into speech.

"Ah, *mon cherie*, my dearest Lady Christina. You are precisely as our darling Mina promised, and as pretty as your sweet mama."

"You knew my mother?"

"*Oui, c'est vrai*, I knew your mama and your papa, but neither so well as your *grand-père*. He maintained a correspondence of long-standing with my own dear departed husband, and his letters were always filled with talk of you. Oh, how proud he was, and now I can see why. You're much more than a mere beauty, you're a bright gel in the mind and soul. Inner beauty, that's what I call it. I can see it in your eyes . . . got a sense of humor, too, and an independent streak." Expressively, she tossed her hands skyward. "Am I right? *C'est vrai?* But what, pray tell, are you doing with so ramshackle a rogue as Ramsey?" There was an undeniable twinkle of merriment in her eyes. It was evident that she was fond of Duncan Ramsey and derived a measure of delight from teasing the gentleman, whom she lectured, "You must not monopolize this *jeune fille* when there are so many other *gentils hommes* who seek an introduction."

"Of course not, ma'am. The Lady Christina is a most" — he paused as if searching for the proper word, then added in an undeniably provocative tone — *"desirable* young lady, and I would not like to be accused of such deplorable conduct."

"Ça c'est bon, we're agreed." She hooked an arm through Tina's and directed her attention to the other side of the ballroom. *"Regardez.* Do you see that gentleman? He is the Marquess of Findon. A most respectable title, profitable estates, and he's been asking about you, *mon cherie.* I shall act as your *grandmère* this evening. It's been a long time since I've been able to play Cupid and introduce young people to one another. What fun we shall have."

"Grandmère," the Earl of Brierly interrupted. "Lady Christina does not know you well enough to have you meddling in her personal affairs."

"Fiddlesticks."

"She will think you a dreadfully managing female."

"And I would not dare to deny it." Ignoring her grandson, she said to Ramsey, "I trust you won't object if Lady Christina comes with me, sir?"

"It sounds an excellent proposition."

"I have always liked you, young man. A rogue you may be, but a wise rogue." She laughed a light sensuous sound reminiscent of the coquettish young lady she had once been.

187

"I shall see to it that Lady Christina enjoys herself and while doing so is proclaimed the toast of the evening. Come, *mon cherie*, first, I shall introduce you to the marquess."

The dowager countess was true to her word, and with a few carefully dropped words the appearance of the reclusive Lady Christina Braughton caused more than the usual stir that occurs when a beautiful lady of mysterious reputation reenters Society. Since the previous Season, Lady Charlotte Spencer had been considered the Town's loveliest, cleverest, and most desirable young miss, but Tina soon eclipsed the reigning beauty. In no time she was the object of everyone's eye and much prying curiosity, and employing the shrewdest discretion, the dowager countess made certain that every word circulated about Tina was naught but of the highest caliber.

"An heiress of vast and independent means," she began in a whispered aside to several bachelors while Tina danced with the Marquess of Findon. Predictably, the gentlemen took note. A beautiful wife was one thing, but when coupled with wealth a lady was irresistible, and soon Tina's dance card was filled.

"Never married because she could afford to wait for love," the dowager countess forged onward, causing many a matron to experience a distinct pang of jealousy. Having each been forced to wed in her first Season, it was impossible for them not to yearn for something more than that first brief infatuation with the notion of marriage, impossible not to wish they might be as blessed as the Lady Christina, who must have evaded the heartache and disappointment they had known.

"And, oh, such a generous girl. *Un très gentil coeur.* Did you know she is raising several orphans? No time for gossip or racing curricles and such fripperies. Why, I do believe good works shall become the rage this Season," the dowager concluded, prompting more than one scheming ingenue to declare that she intended to contribute the bulk of her clothing allowance to the local bettering society.

As the evening progressed Tina became the envy of every lady in attendance and the object of many a gentleman's matrimonial ambition. She danced with a great number of eligible earls and marquesses and was partnered for dinner with the Duke of Beaufort, a widower with four young children, who was thrilled to spend his time with a lady who was not bored with news of his offspring and was herself willing to offer advice on how to maintain harmony among a motherless household.

In no time, she had forgotten her worries, but she had not forgotten Duncan Ramsey, nor the confidences he had shared with her, nor the way he had held her and the disturbing manner he had gazed upon her. She did not understand any of it, and when he offered to drive her back to Cockleshell Manse, she started to refuse, but changed her mind. What harm could there be in letting him take her home? He was her cousin, besides which she had too much sense to let him turn her head. Or so she thought.

"Did you have a good time this evening?" he asked as they settled back against the squabs, side by side in the closed carriage.

"Oh yes. It wasn't at all what I expected when the countess said a small gathering, but that didn't matter, especially not after the dowager countess took charge. She is a unique lady, isn't she? I don't believe I've ever met anyone quite so well meaning and scheming all at once."

He laughed. "Indeed, it's said the marriage of her grandson to Miss O'Kieffe would never have occurred were it not for her timely intervention. She is a lady who always accomplishes her goal."

"Then I have much for which to thank her, for she set out to make my evening a success and quite surpassed herself."

"The dowager countess was a busy lady, but much of that success is yours alone. You were exquisite tonight, and just as the dowager countess said, you reflect an inner and outer beauty that's almost irresistible. Indeed, you conquered many a heart, and the Season's not even launched."

"Are *you* flirting with me, sir?" she asked in a playful voice, wishing there was more light in the carriage so she might better read his expression.

"Flirtation is a finely honed art, my lady, and all too often a form of deception that is nothing but splendid eloquence devoid of truth or substance or sincerity." Smoothly, he reached up to push back the hood of her velvet evening cloak. The meager light within the carriage fell upon her face, and gazing into her eyes, he whispered, "My words are genuine. I do not seek to deceive, merely to speak the truth."

His hands moved upward and his fingers threaded through her hair, brushing it back with infinite gentleness. The coronet of silk lilacs fell backward, and Tina, unable to break away from his intense regard, trembled. His gaze was ardent, making her head feel light and dizzy as if she had consumed too much wine, and a hot unnerving pang pulsed deep in her stomach, marking her awareness of him as a man.

"Don't you remember what I said when you asked if it was all right to waltz? What I said then is true now. I would never lie to you," he said, the velvet warmth of his breath deliciously tickling her neck.

"I shall never forget," came her breathless answer, and as the vehicle slipped into Regent's Park the safe shores of what she had assumed to be fledgling friendship fled into the shadows of the trees. The interior of the carriage darkened to near blackness, his arm went about her waist, and Tina hesitated no more than a fraction of a second, then allowed him to draw her closer.

The swaying of the carriage, so slow, so rhythmic and sensual, the silence that seemed to magnify her shallow breathing to thunderous heights, and his nearness, so close that his heart seemed to beat against hers, were an exhilarating combination. It was as if a stranger had entered her body, and as if giving credulity to the fact that she was losing possession of her wits, she experienced the urge to reach up and touch his face. Tina had never touched a man, never dreamed of doing so until this moment, still she knew how it would feel to run her fingertips down the length of his jaw. It would be hard and lean and a little rough. She shivered and instead of pulling away, she allowed that stranger to control her. She turned in the cradle of his arm, fitting her slender form against his solid chest, then she closed her eyes as a new and unfamiliar, but oh so luscious, warmth began to uncoil within her.

Ramsey inhaled sharply. He could feel the swell of her bosom. Her closeness tantalized him and he could not shut out the memory of that stolen kiss five years before. In his callowness, he had thought that he could take a kiss from the young girl and that would be the end of it, but how wrong he had been. She had smelled of lavender, reminding him of his lost goodness and honesty; her innocence — like wine to a starving man — had been intoxicating, and when she had opened her mouth beneath his desire had stirred within him. The trusting surrender of an innocent was something he had never encountered, and it held the seductive promise of tender passion and total possession.

Now that girl was more than a memory. She was flesh and blood, her soft warm body was pressed against his, rekindling that passion, and he could not help wondering if her kisses would be as sweet as they had been that night so long ago at Almack's.

Just one kiss, he thought, and then he would behave himself. Just one kiss.

Slowly, ever so slowly, Ramsey lowered his lips to brush one velvety sweet caress across her mouth, but when he met Tina's lips, parted as if waiting for his touch, he wanted more. His lips became harder and more demanding. He whispered her name, filling her with a burst of hot urgent breath, and his hands moved upward to cup her head, fingers wrapped about silky strands of hair, as his lips burned a trail across her chin up her cheek to her eyelids and then returned to her mouth.

A throaty little moan escaped Tina. Her head fell back while her body arched forward, and pressing closer to him, she lifted her arms wantonly around his neck. The warmth was everywhere now. She felt like a melting candle and her fingers trembled against his throat. Tina was vaguely aware that something extraordinary was happening to her, something thrilling and frightening and, perhaps, a little dangerous, but his nearness was her one reality. It seemed as if she had been waiting her whole life for this precise moment, and she was not going to let anything so warm and immediate be too quickly extinguished. Her heart raced and again, she moaned beneath her breath, returning his kisses caress for caress.

Ramsey's whole body was prepared for a single ultimate moment. The pliant lips beneath his seemed to urge him on, and he had a sudden vision of what it would be like to make love with this woman. Passion, hot and hard and quick, came to mind, not sweetness or gentleness or anything remotely tender, and stunned by those images, he pulled his lips from hers and raised his head. In the dim light he could see her large eyes searching his and the faint tremor of swollen lips. She was frightened, aroused, and confused.

My God, what's come over me? No sooner had she offered him her trust than he had been about to abuse it. As if to erase what he had done, he drew a shaking hand over his eyes. He knew she was waiting for him to speak, to say anything to explain what had just happened, and even though he knew it had been wrong to kiss her, he would not apologize. To do so was bound to wound her as he had done once before, and this time, it was different. This time, he had wanted to kiss her. God, how he had wanted to kiss her, and he did not regret it for one instant. It had been pleasurable beyond expectation, and he did not wish to ruin this moment for either of them.

Despite an attempt to insert some normalcy into his voice, his words were hoarse when he spoke.

"A relative has some prerogatives, but *that* I

195

assure you is not one of them."

One slim hand fluttered to her throat in a touchingly uncertain gesture. She found her breath suspended and was unable to reply.

"I hope you're not angry with me." His voice was low and intimate. His eyes rested on the vulnerable curve of her mouth.

Tina moistened her lips. The simple truth was Duncan Ramsey was the only man to ever touch her, and the heart-stopping reality was there would never be anyone else. Conveniently, Tina had disguised her true feelings for this man beneath the safe veil of friendship, but it was not friendship she felt; it was something deeper and far more intimate, something that could only be known between a man and a woman. "No. What I feel is far from anger. What I feel is delicious and warm. I think it's the way a woman is supposed to feel," she thought and then gasped as she realized that she had voiced such a revealing thought aloud. Flustered, she closed her eyes.

Her ingenuous words affected Ramsey. Lord, but she was right. The emotions growing between them were not those of cousins or mere friends, but of a man and a woman, and he wanted more than to help solve her problems with the Council. She was a breathtaking and desirable woman, and he wanted her in every way that a man yearns for a woman. In the space of minutes, their relationship had been transformed. One moment they had been on the threshold of friendship, but with that kiss friendship had turned to something far more intimate; with that kiss it seemed as if she belonged to him for all time, and he did not want to merely repay a debt and then walk out of her life. He wanted to make her happy, to spoil her, take care of her, and to make love to her. How so much could have changed in so little time was remarkable. The truth stunned Ramsey, and it was a full minute before he replied.

"Your honesty is a treasure." There was such aching tenderness in his voice that she opened her eyes.

"You understand then?" she asked, her voice trembling with uncertainty.

"Of course I do." He reached out, ran the back of his hand down her cheek, and knew she blushed, for her delicate skin was warm against his. "I'm glad you're not angry, for I would not want to do anything to jeopardize our growing . . . " — he hesitated before saying — "friendship. I've enjoyed the past few weeks more than I can say."

"So have I," she said, her soft voice coming no louder than a whisper as she recognized the truth of this for the first time.

"If I may, I should like to call upon you in the morning. Perhaps you and I might go for a ride. Just the two of us."

"I should like that."

"Until tomorrow then," he said so gently that she felt rather than heard his parting words.

Inside Cockleshell Manse, she leaned against the heavy door and listened to the crunch of carriage wheels as the vehicle rolled down the drive. It was dark and silent and unusually still in the great hall, but she did not feel alone. Wrapping her arms about her waist, Tina smiled at all that had happened this evening. She had waltzed with the earl, she had experienced the heady first stirrings of passion and womanhood, and she had boldly returned his kisses in the carriage, but something even more significant had come to pass.

This night, yesterday, and today had melded into one, and the odious Captain Ramsey was no more. Now there was only the earl, who could be a part of a bright and shining tomorrow.

Nine

The next morning Tina had barely seated the children around the dining room table before several bouquets of flowers were delivered. Reaction was swift, curiosity intense, and despite Tina's entreaty that they remain in their places, the children clambered from their chairs to inspect the admiring notes tucked between vivid blossoms.

Finny retrieved a gilt-edged card from a bouquet of gillyflowers and daffodils and waved it overhead. "This one's from a Lord Tweeddale."

Not an earl? was Tina's silent query.

"And here's one that says, *Your devoted servant, Findon.*"

A tiny frown knit Tina's brow. *Had Ramsey forgotten so soon?*

"Oh, and look at the roses." Lettie made no effort to contain her delight She danced circles about the table brandishing another gilt-edged card in the air. "They're from a duke!"

Of course, Ramsey hadn't forgotten, a confident inner voice reassured Tina. *He intended to bring his bouquet when he came to call as he had promised.*

Hobbins entered the dining room with another armful of flowers, and breakfast deteriorated. Tina was not allowed a single moment to enjoy her shirred egg or sip her morning cocoa. The questions were endless.

"Did you dance?" everyone asked at once.

"Yes, with many fine gentlemen," she replied, but it was Duncan Ramsey's face that came to mind.

"Were they handsome?" demanded Lettie.

"Of course," she said, thinking, *He was the handsomest man there.*

"And did you waltz?"

Oh yes, indeed, I waltzed and it was like walking on air. Tina recalled the blissful moments when Duncan Ramsey's arm had been wrapped about her waist and he had propelled her about the ballroom, yet all she said aloud was a modest, "Yes, I waltzed."

Thus commenced a remarkable day, the next few hours being no less extraordinary as a stream of footmen arrived bearing invitations and more flowers, and by afternoon the knocker upon the massive front door resounded steadily as ladies and gentlemen came to call upon Lady Christina. Never before had there been so many visitors at Cockleshell Manse and that alone would have justified the children's keen interest, but their desire to inspect each guest and to eavesdrop upon every word was heightened by the fact that it was none other than their own darling Tina mum who had captured the attention of Society. Francis and Finny hung from the ancient oak tree at the head of the drive, taking careful note of the crest upon each arriving vehicle; Joshua, determined to protect Tina from fortune hunters or other rascals of dishonorable intent, lurked in the corridor between the great hall and the Winter Saloon, where Tina was receiving; Lettie, intent upon cataloging the wardrobe of each female visitor and the color of each gentleman's eyes, peered through the windows from the flagged terrace; the smaller girls, somewhat bewildered by this spate of activity, observed the comings and goings from the musicians' balcony. None of this was precisely circumspect, and only when their new friend Miss Penny was appointed official delegate to the saloon, having been given strict orders to commit every last syllable of conversation to memory, did the children abandon their posts and retire to the schoolroom.

The fifth tray of sweetmeats was being circulated around the room. The sugar cakes had been consumed, and the bulk of the visitors had already come, paid their respects to Lady Christina, engaged in idle chatter about the merits of Town weather versus the country, dropped juicy *on dits* about the approaching Season and whose name was bound to be linked with whose, and then departed, having confined their visit to the socially acceptable fifteen minutes. The Duke of Beaufort and the Marquess of Findon remained, both gentlemen being determined to be the final focus of Lady Christina's attention that afternoon. Their goal was, however, crushed when Hobbins announced another visitor.

"Lord Tweeddale," he intoned, then hurried off to the pantry for more refreshments.

At this development, Penelope, who had been politely listening to the marquess ramble on about his ailing mother, emitted a tiny squeak, jumped up from the brocaded Louis XIV chair upon which she had been sitting, spun around in search of escape, and darted behind the nearest length of peacock blue velvet curtain.

Everyone else looked toward the door.

"Lord Tweeddale, what a pleasure it is to welcome you to Cockleshell Manse." Although Tina offered the standard social smile, she was not as collected as she appeared. Once again she could not help wondering why Duncan Ramsey had not yet arrived as he had promised, and she could not repress the thought that perhaps she had once again made a fool of herself where that particular gentleman was concerned.

"Thank you, my lady," his lordship said, noting with annoyance that both of the chairs nearest to Lady Christina were occupied. He acknowledged Beaufort and Findon with the sort of nod that could hardly be qualified as civil, but neither gentleman seemed to notice or care.

"I say, Lady Christina, where did your charming young friend disappear to?" inquired the marquess, who had just begun to describe how the doctor leeched his mother on alternate Wednesdays and was eager to tout the praises of his mama's latest physician.

Behind the curtain the errant young miss flattened herself against the paneled wall.

Tina glimpsed about the room. "I've no idea. She was here a moment ago."

"A friend?" Deciding that this must be his lucky day after all, his lordship's sour expression brightened. Although he had ventured out to Cockleshell Manse in the hopes of seducing Lady Christina, he was not finicky; if the friend was half as pretty or half as well settled as Lady Christina, then she would do just as nicely.

"Yes, and a fetching girl she was. Quiet and

well mannered. Good listener," expanded Findon. "Fact is she reminds me of someone, though I can't say who. Name's Miss Penny, and she's up from the country. New to Town."

"Penny?" Lord Tweeddale mused aloud. "I'm not familiar with the name."

"Never thought you were such a high stickler," rejoined the duke. "What's in a name, I say? Gel's under the sponsorship of Lady Christina and that's all that matters."

Having the decency to feel a tad chastised, Lord Tweeddale moderated his tone. "I would like to have met the young lady," he said, trying for as cordial a tenor as he could manage.

But Penelope recognized *that* tone of voice, and she knew that whatever he was thinking was far from cordial. Ned was a barracuda of the first degree, and it was more than likely that he was really saying, "I'd like the chance to give her the once-over, then try to inveigle whatever I might out of her."

It was a discouraging thing to have so insensitive and avaricious a sibling, and forgetting where she was, Penelope dropped her head in sadness. The curtain rustled, and she held her breath, praying that no one noticed the movement. In the next instant, her worries multiplied twofold.

Another voice drifted in from the corridor, and Penelope almost fainted from shock.

"Thank you, Hobbins, I can let myself in."

Great Jupiter, it was the Earl of Croick! What was he doing here? Penelope wondered, wishing that she could see where he was standing and what was going on in the saloon.

On the other side of the curtain all eyes were upon the lady and the earl. Their waltz had not gone unnoticed, nor had their departure at the end of the evening, and although it was known they were cousins even the most simple-minded soul could not avoid delving for a bit of intrigue. No one wished to cast aspersions upon the lady, but Ramsey's reputation was infamous, and even the duke engaged in a moment of uncharitable speculation as to the real nature of their relationship.

"Good afternoon, my lord," said Lady Christina, turning her brightest smile of the day upon this latest caller. Ramsey was here at last, precisely as he said he would be, and she could not help noticing how fine he appeared in a coat of Bath-blue superfine and his cravat tied à la Irish. Unequivocally, he was the handsomest and most fascinating man she had ever known. Truth to tell, life had been quite tedious until their collision that afternoon in the park.

For the space of a moment, his eyes met

hers, and in response, her smile reached near celestial proportions. "Lady Christina, you look as enchanting as ever," Ramsey greeted, managing to keep the surprise and disappointment from his voice. Given her success last evening, it was natural that her saloon would be flooded with gentlemen, but he was nonetheless displeased by the admiring covey clustered about her, particularly by the presence of Tweeddale. There was so much he wished to say to her. Last evening, a bond of trust had been forged between them, and today, he had intended to speak of his efforts in her behalf regarding the Council. Indeed, he quite fancied the notion of being her hero. With a bow, he handed her an enormous bouquet of gardenias mixed with Holland tulips of deep lilac.

"How exquisite." And with no intention of slighting the other gentlemen, who had sent flowers, she added in innocence, "They're the most beautiful flowers I've ever received."

The duke, who was a good-natured sort of fellow, paid no heed to this remark, but the marquess, on the other hand, who seldom resorted to flowers to win a lady's attention, was miffed. Lord Tweeddale, needless to say, was vastly put out; he had been forced to do business with an odious gullgroper to pay for the flowers and he abhorred wasting blunt unless it was on a game of hazard or a night at the Pigeon Hole. In his case, the bouquet was a monumental waste of funds, and his lordship stared daggers at his friend.

As she arranged the gardenias and tulips in a vase, Tina addressed Ramsey, "We were discussing my guest, Miss Penny. It's a shame she has disappeared for I'm certain she would have enjoyed meeting you, my lord."

"I didn't know you had a guest. You never mentioned it before."

"Been keeping tabs on your cousin's every moment?" Lord Tweeddale queried on a wheedling underbreath.

Ramsey, his visage darkening rapidly, directed a reproving eye upon his friend.

"Miss Penny arrived rather unexpectedly," explained Tina, choosing to ignore his lordship and hoping that he would have the decency to leave when the socially prescribed visiting period had expired.

The duke made a coughing sort of noise that indicated imminent speech and the other occupants of the room looked in his direction. "It's a mild spring we've been having. Don't you agree? Today, for example. Can't remember last time we had such a run of unseasonably warm days in March," he remarked in an offhand tone, having made the momentous decision to take the plunge and endeavor to separate Lady Christina from the other gentlemen by inviting her for a stroll in her garden. How was he to tell her of the latest woes with his eldest daughter, if Findon continued to monopolize her attention with that revolting account of his mother and her maladies? Or worse, if Tweeddale and Ramsey, for reasons known to no one other than themselves, resorted to fisticuffs in the lady's saloon?

"Indeed, it's an ideal day for a ride in the park," said the marquess, grateful that the duke had laid the groundwork for his own play to gain the lady's undivided attention. "How about it, Lady Christina? Are you game? My carriage is right outside."

"I say," put in Lord Tweeddale, finding it unbelievable that he had more than one besotted fool with which to deal. He would be damned if he let the flowers be a total waste. "I had the exact notion, myself. Ideal afternoon for an outing."

Ramsey intervened with a confident grin. "That's all well and good, but, you see, gentlemen, my cousin and I had already made arrangements for the afternoon."

Tina shot him a glance from under her thick lashes, and her mind went back to that kiss in the carriage. She remembered how his hand had stroked across her cheek, how hot and hard and demanding his lips had been upon hers, and she recalled the delicious inner warmth that had uncoiled within her as she pressed closer to his chest. A fiery pink tinted her cheeks, for the mere memory of those intimate moments caused that melting sensation to begin anew. With an unwavering gaze, Ramsey studied her flushed countenance, a wicked grin turned up at the corners of his mouth, and she knew beyond a doubt that he, too, was thinking of their kiss.

"I say, Ramsey, we were here first," Lord Tweeddale blurted out.

"May I remind you, Ned, that Lady Christina is not a prime piece of horseflesh, nor are we taking numbers and waiting in line for a loaf of bread."

"Didn't mean that," he retorted, a calculating expression forming upon his countenance. "Besides I can't fathom why *you'd* be calling and bringing flowers. After all, it's not as if you're — "

"Why don't we all go," Ramsey cut him short. Being one of four escorts was not what he would have liked, but neither did he wish to have Lady Christina hear whatever Ned had been about to say.

Tina, too, knew a pang of disappointment; still her smile was gracious. "That's a splendid solution, and I fancy I shall be the envy of every lady in the park." As she rose all four gentlemen converged upon her person to offer an arm, and a ripple of laughter spilled forth from her lips. Although she would rather have spent the afternoon with no one other than Duncan Ramsey, she was delighted by the purely feminine thrill of enjoyment she derived from being surrounded by so many ardent gentlemen at one time.

Penelope came out of her hiding place, plopped herself on the nearest sofa, and swiped at a dusty cobweb hanging across her forehead like an errant lock of hair. What a coil she had landed herself in. Cockleshell Manse was no safe harbor from Ned and the earl. It presented a morass of pitfalls at every turn, and it was bound to be sooner rather than later that she tumbled into one of those pits. There was no time to dillydally about Town in search of her beloved. This called for drastic measures; she had to seek out Cook to enlist her immediate assistance. Mayhap there was some charm to induce the appearance of her beloved.

The boys, who had quit the schoolroom at the sound of the departing carriage, told Penelope that Cook had taken Diana and Mary Katherine for a walk beside the canal, and Penelope hurried outside in search of the woman. As she walked along the pebbled path, a gentleman rounded the corner of the house. Tall and fair-haired, it was none other than Mr. O'Kieffe and he was coming straight toward her.

"Lady Christina has gone out," Penelope snapped. She was cross as crabs. Mr. O'Kieffe was the last person she wished to see at this precise moment.

He touched the brim of his curly beaver hat and made a short bow. "But I did not come to see Lady Christina. I came to see you, Miss Penny."

"Well, you can't stay, if I'm unchaperoned, and I am. So that's that. Besides, I have business to attend to. I was searching for Cook." She turned and sauntered off, giving him the benefit of her back.

"Fine." He dashed several paces ahead of her to gain her attention and smiled, the most maddening, irresistible smile Penelope had ever beheld. "I'll come with you and when we find Cook she can be your chaperon."

"You're an exceedingly domineering gentleman," said Penelope, wishing that he was not so devastatingly good looking. It would be much easier to ignore him if he were hunchbacked and forty pounds heavier. But that was not the case, and it required every ounce of fortitude to continue walking down the path.

"Domineering, you say?" There was that infuriating grin again. "So I've been told."

"And stubborn and arrogant."

"And very much entranced by you, Miss Penny."

"And far too bold!" She tossed an accusing glance over her shoulder.

His green eyes twinkled. "Yes, that as well."

"Aha, so you admit I'm not the first female to entrance you."

"No, nothing of the sort. I admit that I've been called bold."

"And exasperating, too," Penelope shot back for good measure.

Reaching out to touch her forearm, his voice was suddenly serious. "Why are you trying to avoid me?"

Unable to control the impulse, she stopped and turned around partway until her eyes met his. "Why shouldn't I?"

"Because I'm not here to trifle with you, Miss Penny. I'm here owing to a sincere desire to get to know you," he said in such a way that her heart contracted and she wondered for one mad moment if she had committed the unpardonable transgression of falling in love with someone she barely knew, a someone who was, moreover, not the gentleman Madame Zaborini had seen in the tea leaves.

"There's not much to know." Penelope resumed walking, but her pace was slower than before and her back was not quite so stiff.

"You must let me be the judge of that." He lengthened his stride so that he walked beside her. "Have you a large family, Miss Penny?"

"No. There's just myself and my older brother."

"Ah, well, I'm a brother and know all about brothers and sisters. Is he dreadfully overprotective?"

"Not really. Despotic is a better word."

At this sober turn in the conversation, he was moved to ask, "What of your parents?"

"My mother died when I was an infant, and Papa was centuries older than most fathers," she said as if talking with Mr. O'Kieffe were the most natural thing in the world. "He died before I was four, so I never really knew him."

"At least, you've got your brother, and at least, he's given the matter of your future some serious consideration."

Thrown into confusion, Penelope cast a sideways peek at Mr. O'Kieffe. What on earth was he talking about? Certainly, he did not know who she was or that Ned had arranged her wedding to the earl.

"I was merely assuming, that is. He sent

you to Lady Christina for the Season, and having done so is evidence of his concern." But even as he spoke, Mr. O'Kieffe knew this was not the truth. It was revealed in the sad way her shoulders slumped and the brave little smile she forced upon her lips. Whoever this girl's brother was the fellow did not give a tinker's damn for her welfare. O'Kieffe thought of his gambling cronies and the fast set of young bucks who frequented London's hells, and it was with genuine sympathy that he wondered which selfish clout was her brother. He could be the Earl of Rosebery or Lord Henry Manners or that Tweeddale chap, to name a few. The list was endless, and it actually did not matter who; it mattered only that the man had probably never entertained a thought for his sister unless it was to consider how he might make a profit off her. Reality was too grim, and so he teased, "Don't tell me he's an ogre with pockets to let and has sold you to the highest bidder to save the family seat."

"Of course not," she whispered, but the pinched expression upon her face told him otherwise. She halted. They had reached the end of the path. Cook was nowhere in sight, and blindly, Penelope stared at the muddy waters of the canal.

Yes, Miss Penny was a damsel in distress,

and although this was nothing novel to Mr. O'Kieffe, the fierceness of his reaction to this particular damsel was new. The urge to take her in his arms and shield her against the world defied all logic. Softly, he said, "I should like to be your friend."

"Truly?" She stared up at him.

"Truly. I should like to visit you and get to know you, and when you like you may tell me the whole of it, and perhaps, I can help. That's what friends are for, you know." Without further ado, he took her hand in his and briefly he allowed his lips to touch the bare flesh of the back of her hand; then he let it drop, bowed, and retreated, having been naught but a perfect gentleman.

Penelope remained by the canal, watching his retreating figure, and it was not until he disappeared around the corner of the house that she allowed herself to exhale the massive pent-up breath she had been holding since he kissed her hand.

She was in love! Oh, there was no doubt about it, and it was a disaster. Not only was her heart beating at an unconscionable pace, but she was sporting the poppy pink outfit she had intended to wear when she encountered her beloved. All signs pointed to an unmitigated calamity.

On the verge of tears, she scurried off in

search of Cook, hoping against all odds there was some spell or infusion that could turn back the foolish course of one's heart. Why, she would even resort to eating a dozen roses and sleeping with a rotten orange under her arm, or was it eating an orange and sleeping with roses? Whichever, it did not matter, for Penelope was bound and determined to do whatever was necessary to put her life in order without delay.

Over the next few days the pattern of activity at Cockleshell Manse continued in the same vein. The beau monde continued to make the less than fashionable trip out to Regent's Park to pay their respects upon Lady Christina, for the Season was soon to begin and no one wished to be *du vieux temps* when it came to the Town's latest and most desirable *partie*. The company was endless, enough *oolong souchang* had been served to float a navy, scones and jellied sandwiches had been consumed in quantities more appropriate to sustaining an army, and Cook and Hobbins, having found it impossible to simultaneously answer the door, announce visitors, serve refreshments, and prepare more edibles, had resorted to hiring two maids, a scullery assistant, and a footman. The children, of course, were undaunted by the inconvenience and persisted in thinking the hubbub was, in Finny's words, *all the kick*, but Lady Christina did not agree. Social success, it appeared, had as many shortcomings as did failure; this was not the new and perfect future she had envisioned for herself, for Duncan Ramsey was seldom a part of it at all.

Not once since the countess's party had Tina had the opportunity to visit with Duncan Ramsey as she had become used to doing, and on more than one occasion she recalled those intimate moments in the carriage and entertained the improper thought: When would she ever get to be *alone* with him again?

It was always one visitor or another, and on this particular afternoon it was the Countess of Brierly, the dowager countess, and Mr. Cadwallader, the only persons, aside from the earl, whose company she welcomed.

"*Vraiment, monsieur,* it is a pleasure to meet you at last," the dowager countess said to Mr. Cadwallader. "Lady Christina has told us of her plight and of your gallant offer to assist her."

Cadwallader flushed an unbecoming shade of scarlet. It was rare that he found himself in the presence of a genuinely grand lady, and he had never expected to be treated with such kindness. "I fear, however, my assistance has been of little value, for I bring un-

217

fortunate news today."

Tina placed her teacup on a nearby table and sat forward. The grave look upon Mr. Cadwallader's countenance was most nerve-racking. "You must tell me, sir, what has happened?"

"Silas Barnaby visited my office, and it appears the Council has located a magistrate willing to consider an eviction notice."

The ladies gasped, but none as loud as Tina, who feared she might swoon.

"*Oh, mon dieu! Quele dommage.* What is this world coming to, I ask? It is beyond the bounds of disgraceful," declared the dowager in outrage. "And who is this Silas Barnaby person? I shall see him posthaste."

Mr. Cadwallader raised a hand in clarification. "Mind you, my lady, I merely said *willing* to consider. The magistrate has not yet agreed to their demands."

"Not yet," said Tina in a dispirited tone of voice. "But he shall."

"Ah, no! It is not true. *Ce n'est pas vrais.* And we shall not give up, little one," the dowager countess informed Tina optimistically.

"Well stated, my lady," Mr. Cadwallader agreed with such a forceful nod that his spectacles slid down the length of his nose. His complexion reddening once again, he pushed them back up.

"Have you a plan, sir?" inquired the dowager.

"Indeed, I do, but it is a bit unusual and unconventional."

"Ah, but how else to fight so outlandish a situation than with the unconventional. Come, you must tell us, sir. *Immediatement!*"

Bolstered by the dowager's support, Cadwallader related his plan. "We must find a gentleman of the highest rank, a gentleman with funds and social account and power and thus, the ability to intimidate the Council, and we must get him to agree to announce his betrothal to Lady Christina."

"*Magnifique!* I comprehend the direction of your thoughts, sir, and it is a brilliant notion. What you propose, I assume, is a sham engagement to stave off the Council. A betrothal to someone that no magistrate in the realm would dare to cross."

"Precisely."

"*Monsieur, sans doute je crois que vous êtes un homme très intelligent. Vous êtes brilliant et un bon ami.*"

Although Mr. Cadwallader did not comprehend a single word of French, he grinned, pleased that his notion had met with such hearty endorsement. But, in the opposite chair, the Countess of Brierly did not look so certain, and as for Tina, she was entirely in doubt about the scheme.

"Oh, your Mr. Cadwallader is brilliant. Don't you agree?" the dowager raved, ignoring the horrified expression upon Tina's countenance. "Now who shall it be? Beaufort? No. Doubtless he would take the whole matter far too seriously and wish to marry you in the end, and we would not want that, for remember, a lady must marry only for love. But a betrothal here or there, well, what harm could there be in that, *n'est-ce pas?*"

"But, ma'am," began Tina, unable to discern how she had lost control of the situation.

"No, no, no!" The dowager stabbed the air with a finger. "There will be no buts and no worries. This is a splendid plan, and I know just how to reach our goal. You shall have a party, Lady Christina, and we'll invite all of the best candidates to attend. You may meet them and then make a decision. Mr. Cadwallader, I see a desk." She pointed across the room and instructed, "Sir, bring me a pencil and some paper, *s'il vous plaît.* We must begin making the guest list."

Tina turned to the countess for assistance, but the younger woman waved her hands airily. "When *Grandmère* gets a notion there's no stopping her, and I fear this is one of those times. We've no choice but to cooperate. Besides, it does sound like it might work, and there's no harm in trying. *Grandmère*, don't forget to invite the twins. Though not titled, they've the power and sort of connections that might be of value."

Penelope, who had been woolgathering in the window seat, was at last shaken from her daydream. "Twins?" she inquired in a pitch of high excitement at mention of the word she had been pondering for days.

"Yes, my brothers. Michael and Kevin."

"Do you mean the Mr. O'Kieffe who comes to call? That Mr. O'Kieffe is a twin?"

"He is."

"And do they look alike?" She was sounding more bird-witted than usual.

"*Naturellement*," put in the dowager, most impatient to get back to planning Lady Christina's party. "Of course, they look alike. Most twins do."

Whereupon Penelope let forth an ungovernable burst of giggles and rushed from the room.

"That was most peculiar," said Tina after the girl had left.

The dowager agreed. "Never encountered such a fleabrain in all my days. Poor gel . . . weak bloodlines, no doubt." She shook her head. "Something familiar about her, though I can't quite place it."

Tina chewed her lower lip in consternation.

Should she tell the truth about Miss Penny? No, she decided, she had already burdened her friends with enough of her personal problems. There was no reason why she should not be able to handle the impetuous Miss Penny on her own. And so Tina, for the umpteenth time, let a chance to confide in someone about Miss Penny pass.

Upstairs in the schoolroom Penelope broke into whoops of sheer jubilation and danced about the room with Finny. She was blathering about twins and Mr. O'Kieffe and a gypsy and rotten oranges, and the children, having not the vaguest idea what she was saying, stared at her as if she were the village idiot.

"Oh, don't you see? It's all right after all. I shan't have to marry the earl. I'm going to marry Mr. O'Kieffe."

To which she received a perplexed frown from young Finny. Considering how she had been hiding from Mr. O'Kieffe every time he came to call, the proposition was beyond belief. Miss Jane was an awfully nice girl, but there was no doubt that she was a bit queer at times, and this, Finny decided, was one of those times. Miss Penny marry Mr. O'Kieffe? Why, one would think the Fates had dictated her future the way she was acting so downright certain.

Ten

"I had quite despaired of ever sharing another evening with you and the children," said Ramsey. Lifting his wineglass, he toasted Tina and smiled around the table at the children. "May we enjoy many more companionable gatherings such as this."

Tina returned his smile. "I believe we have the weather to thank for this evening."

"To the weather," Ramsey rejoined with another lift of his goblet.

It had rained steadily since the dowager countess's visit two days before, turning the road through Regent's Park into a sea of mud and causing an abrupt cessation of the visits to Cockleshell Manse. Only Duncan Ramsey had braved the storm. He had come to call this afternoon, bearing flowers for Lady Christina, foreign coins for the boys, pink ribbon candy for the girls, and, of course, a special doll for Diana. He had arrived too late for tea, and readily, he had accepted their invitation to stay for dinner.

"You must tell me about your young visitor," he said conversationally. "Where is the mysterious Miss Penny this evening?"

"She has a beau," divulged Lettie, affecting the sort of blasé tone that was meant to imply vast familiarity with all aspects of courtship. "And Cook says it must be true love to have braved the rain to go and meet his brother."

"She must be quite a paragon," Ramsey said to the girl, his expression gravely intent. "Just imagine, introductions to a young man's brother and not even presented to the whole of Society."

"Oh, she never really came here to be presented to anyone," blurted out Francis, who was beginning to feel annoyed that Lettie was monopolizing the earl with such a trivial topic as Miss Penny's romantic success.

"But I was given to understand she was here for the Season under Lady Christina's sponsorship."

"Oh, no, we rescued her from footpads," expanded Francis. Pleased to have gained the earl's attention, the lad launched into a detailed and highly colorful account of how he and Finny and Joshua had dropped out of the trees to rescue Miss Penny.

"What an extraordinary tale." Ramsey's left brow arched in astonishment and he glanced toward Tina for confirmation.

"The story is completely true, and though you may think it most irresponsible of me, I must confess we're harboring a runaway." Tina related the remainder of the story regarding Miss Penny's arrival at Cockleshell Manse, after which she concluded, "It seemed far wiser to allow her to stay than to send her away to roam the city on her own. I do hope you understand."

"Of course, and I would not have expected any less of you, my lady." His eyes were warm with admiration, and his gentle tone was like a caress. "You have a singularly kind and generous heart, and the young lady was most fortunate to have stumbled into your care."

Delicate shell pink tinted Tina's cheeks. "I did tell her that I would not remain quiet should I hear of anyone searching for a missing daughter or ward. Do you know of such a case?"

Shaking his head in the negative, he suggested, "Perhaps, if you tell me a little about her I might recognize her."

"She's exceedingly lively," exclaimed Finny. "Why, the other day she danced about the schoolroom with me. Likes to whoop a lot, too."

"And she's brave, oh so brave, for she refused to give her reticule to the thieves." Admiration was evident in Lettie's awestruck voice.

225

"You should have seen how she screamed and kicked and fought like a mad boar."

"And she believes in fortunes and gypsies and tea leaves and the Fates just like Cook."

Ramsey rubbed his chin in thought. "Can't say I'm acquainted with any young lady who fits that list of qualities."

Tina laughed at his understated description of Miss Penny. "A sad romp is what Hobbins calls her."

"Ah, the incorrigible type. My guess is that a desperate parent threatened to consign her to a convent and she took flight before the dreadful deed might be done."

"You're nearly on the mark. It was an arranged marriage — which our Miss Penny deems just as gruesome as entering the orders — that precipitated her flight." Everyone laughed at this, and when they had settled down, Tina added, "You shall let me know if you hear anything?"

"Of course. You need not ask."

"I suppose we shall unravel the mystery before long."

"Yes, you're bound to," agreed Ramsey.

Following a festive dessert of sugar puff pyramids — flavored with cocoa in the earl's honor — the meal was done, and the children departed for their rooms, having extracted a promise from the earl that he would come upstairs to say good night, and if they were good, he would read them a story.

"Shall we retire to the library?" suggested Tina. "I believe Hobbins has set a fresh fire."

"That would be nice." He followed her down the corridor and into the cozy room.

Outside, rain slashed against the windows. A bolt of lightning ripped a jagged edge across the night sky and from a distance came the rumbling echo of thunder. Tina pulled the heavy curtains across the windows; the sounds of the storm were muffled, and Ramsey smiled as she turned around to face him. She looked breathtaking tonight. Delicate color was brushed upon her cheeks, soft hair framed her face, and her great round eyes sparkled with affection and trust and yes, an undeniable hint of passion. A lilac garland, he thought, recalling the floral wreath presented to military heroes, and he knew that no accolade would ever be so cherished as the sentiments reflected in those magnificent lilac-colored eyes.

On impulse he went to stand beside her, bent his head, and covered her lips with his own. It was a quick kiss, sweet and warm and tender, but his smile was a roguish one, provocative and heated.

"The prerogative of a relative," he whispered and was rewarded by the delightful

227

deepening of color along her cheekbones.

Tina raised a hand to her warm cheek. Her heart fluttered madly. She was alone with him, but what was it she intended to do with a man who had once been her foe, then a friend and now . . . What was he? Someone to trust? Yes. Someone who had a genuine concern for her and the children? Yes. And then it hit her. Mr. Cadwallader's strategy to outwit the Council was not so farfetched after all. In fact, Duncan Ramsey was exactly the sort of man the dowager countess would choose to help her out of her dilemma. It was such an obvious solution. Why hadn't anyone thought of him right away?

"Sir, I've a tremendous favor to ask of you."

"Nothing could be too large. You know, I would do anything for you," he replied, hoping that he was not going to be asked to deal with the rag-mannered Miss Penny in some sort of fatherly fashion.

Nervous, Tina took one step backward and sat upon the settee. The earl remained standing, looking down at her, his kind expression encouraging her to say, "I'm confronted with a problem that I don't seem to be able to solve on my own." There, she had said it, thereby relinquishing her independence and control. It was done, and although she did not like it in

228

the least, it had not been as painful or as shattering as she had imagined it would be. She went on, "My neighbors in Park Village East have taken it upon themselves to institute a sort of code of conduct that most unwittingly I've broken at every turn."

"I know."

"You do?"

"Yes. Mr. Cadwallader told me the afternoon I took the children to the museum."

"But you did not say a word."

"It was none of my business. Oh, that's not to say I didn't wish to help you, but I suspected that you wished to handle your own affairs. Was I right?"

"Yes, you were right." She smiled at how well this gentleman knew her. "But I'm failing miserably."

"I wouldn't say that. From time to time, we all confront circumstances that are out of control, and this is one of those times. To have tried and failed is nothing to be ashamed of. And I must say that I'm flattered that you've decided to enlist my aid. How can I help?"

Even though Tina was convinced that her imminent request was both necessary and appropriate, she required several seconds to muster her courage to reply. Proposing to a gentleman was not something a young lady did every day, and Tina took a deep breath before beginning, "I must get married, you see, or at least, become betrothed to a gentleman of rank and power whom the Council would not dare to cross, and I was hoping you might agree to be that gentleman."

Of all the things Ramsey had expected Tina to say this was not one of them. Unable to face her, his gaze dropped to the floor, and he threaded both hands through his hair. Oh, God, what had he done? What selfish fantasy had he allowed himself to enjoy about this lady when he knew very well there could be nothing to it? He was already betrothed, and yet, he had conveniently managed to brush that fact from his conscious mind whenever he visited Cockleshell Manse. An unspeakable chill cut through Ramsey. It was as if every last ounce of blood had drained from his mortal self, and with an awful mounting dread he forced himself to raise his head and look at Tina. She was waiting for his reply, and her upturned face revealed her emotions. The unsteady tilt of her chin told of fear, and looking into her eyes, he saw an unmistakable glimmer of hope. His heart gave a lurch.

"Oh, Tina, you must forgive me, but I can't help," he said in a hushed voice, using her Christian name for the first time. "I cannot marry you."

She felt as if the air had been punched from

her lungs, and one slender hand gripped the arm of the settee for support. How could he refuse her? "But it need not be a real marriage. I do not mean to entrap you, sir, or force you into a life that is not of your own choosing. Nothing more than a betrothal of convenience is required until such a time as the Council finds something or someone else to occupy their attention."

"I cannot do even that."

"But I thought we were friends. I thought we were — " She could not continue. The expression upon her face turned bleak, her complexion paled. At length, she added so softly that he had to lean forward to catch her words, "I do not understand."

"How I wish I might say yes, but I can't, and I know you shall never forgive me for treating you in such an unworthy manner," he said with awful dignity.

Thinking that it must be the episode at Almack's of which he spoke, she said, "There is nothing to forgive. I have known all along who you were, and there are but two things to be said of that unfortunate incident. First, we are both much changed in the past five years, and second, as I do not believe in looking backward, there is nothing to forgive."

"Oh, no, my dear lady, there is much to forgive, for sadly, there is much to hold against me. Indeed, it is unforgivable to hurt the same lady twice in a lifetime." Overcome with shame, he once more looked away, then rushed into speech, "I cannot marry you, nor feign an engagement, for I am already betrothed to another."

"Betrothed?" she repeated in horrified disbelief. "How can that be possible?"

"To Tweeddale's sister."

"But you did not say a word. No one did. I don't understand."

"I did not mean to deceive you. At first, it did not seem important, then later on when I avoided mention of her it was because, well, the truth is, if I was deceiving anyone it was myself." He recalled that afternoon in the Winter Saloon and the moment he had cut off Lord Tweeddale in midsentence. Though he had pretended not to know why he did so, the shameful fact was that he had feared the truth. Now he owed it to Tina to tell her all. "It was not a love match, you see, and although I did not admit so aloud, I had begun to realize that a sensible match was not going to be enough for me."

He made a derisive sound, half laugh, half snort, his mind flashing back to that conversation with Durham at the club. *That's all? There's nothing more between you?* the viscount had asked when Ramsey had said, *I'm sure I*

232

couldn't want for a more perfect wife.

"But I was wrong about many things, and it was you, Lady Christina, who showed me what a misguided fool I've been."

"Me?"

"Yes. Too late did I realize what was happening between us." He paused as emotion welled within him. Although he could not voice his feelings, the truth was that what he felt for Tina was what the viscount had been talking about. This aching tenderness mingled with passion and affection was something he never thought to feel for another human being. He drew a hand across his eyes in a gesture of despair. If only he had listened to Durham. If only he had recognized how special Tina was the first time he had set eyes upon her. If only he had walked back into her life last year — before Penelope. In a cheerless tone, he said, "I now know the folly of such a marriage, but it's too late. The fact remains that I'm betrothed to Miss Latham."

The walls of the library spun about Tina. Tears swam before her line of vision. The earl seemed far away, as if viewed through the wrong end of a telescope, and she struggled to focus upon him as he knelt on the carpet before her.

"Please, hear me out." He raised two fingers and held them before her lips. "My sole justification for what has happened between us these past weeks is that our time together, yours and mine as well as mine with your children, has been the most wondrous of my life. At last, I had those brothers and sisters I had yearned for as a boy, and I had you and your generous spirit and gentle humor, your kindness and the radiant vision of your beauty at the other end of the table. I believe I even came to think of Cockleshell Manse as my home, for I knew you would be here, waiting and pleased to welcome me no matter what. I'll not deny that it was wrong and selfish of me to take when I could give nothing in return, but I didn't want it to end." He watched as a single tear slipped from the corner of one shimmering lilac eye. Something tightened about his chest, and he reached up to wipe away the tear from her pale cheek.

"My dearest lady, you mean more to me than words can express, and though I know you may not choose to believe me, it's true. What began as friendship became something else, something infinitely more precious, and I shall cherish that memory for the rest of my days."

Silence fell upon the room as Tina absorbed the full meaning of Ramsey's stunning admission. He was saying the words she had longed to hear. It was not merely friendship that had

blossomed between them but something p[...]
cious, yet he was also telling her he was no[...]
free and that those feelings were wrong. The
truth was a terrible thing to accept, made even
worse by the fact that he was speaking in such
final terms.

"We must part then," she said, a note of
finality in her suddenly small voice.

"I fear there is no other way for it."

"Forever."

"Yes, forever," he agreed, knowing there
was no way he could be in the same room and
not desire her, that there was no way he could
turn back time so that a friendship, safe and
pristine, was all that they felt for one another,
and knowing that above all else that he did not
wish to hurt or dishonor her again.

She cast her eyes down to her lap, then
back up again to gaze into his. Tears shown
like silver raindrops upon her lashes. "I shall
miss you."

Ramsey's breath caught raggedly in his
throat. "And I shall miss you."

Again, she bent her head.

"I did not wish this, and if you never find it
in your heart to forgive me, at least you must
believe that. Once I intentionally used you
and though I achieved the same lamentable
outcome again, please, believe that I never set
out to do so."

There was no mistaking the anguish in his voice, and the realization of his suffering was more than Tina could bear. She clapped her hands to her ears. A steady path of tears was beginning to trickle down her cheeks.

He reached out and caressed her cheek with his thumb, allowing the tears to flow into his hand. "If I could take away your pain and make it mine, I would," he said in utter sincerity, but knowing the uselessness of his words. They were no better than hollow platitudes.

Of a sudden, Tina was immeasurably tired. "You must go now." Her voice was frightfully unsteady, each word was mixed with a great gulp of air.

Leave now? The finality of this moment was devastating to consider, and something within Ramsey protested. *But if I leave, she will be alone again — the children will be alone.* Who would drive up to Rugby with Joshua when he goes off for his first semester? Who would introduce him to the masters and warn him about the peculiar ways of the Latin tutor? What about Diana's first birthday? And how would she explain any of this to the children? he wondered, facing the fact that he had hurt them as well and knowing that the last honorable thing he could do was leave without further ado. He rose. "I shall leave, my lady, but farewell is too final a word. Might I instead say *au revoir?*"

"I should like that," she whispered. Only the ghost of a smile remained upon her lips. "*Au revoir*, my lord."

"*Au revoir*, my lady."

Then he strode out the door and was gone, and as she had done once before Tina went to stand on the threshold of Cockleshell Manse to watch as Duncan Ramsey departed, except this time she knew he would never return. This time, she knew she was not so wise to have prevented herself from falling in love.

For a long time after his carriage disappeared into a bank of fog, she remained on the stoop, standing in the cold wet night and staring at the nothingness. Rain slashed out of the black sky. Wind buffeted her slender figure, her face was white and set, and she shivered. That was all that was left of the hopes and dreams she had had for herself and the children and Cockleshell Manse. Nothingness as bleak as the night. She had always been on her own, but now she was imprisoned, and loneliness, tangible and physical and painful, encircled her like a strangling cloak.

A sennight passed. The weather, matching Tina's mood, continued to be gray. Try as she might, she did not feel up to receiving visitors, nor participating in gay times with the children, who were left in charge of Penelope and the nursery maid. During this period, flowers and notes from well-wishers besieged the house, but no one, owing to the inclement weather and fear of Lady Christina's mysterious and persistent malaise, came to call.

It was late in the afternoon of the seventh day following Ramsey's revelation that Cook sought out Tina who was cloistered in the small sitting room adjacent to her bedchamber. A scattering of fashion plates, a discarded copy of Miss Austen's *Northanger Abbey*, and the latest issues of *La Belle Assemblée* and *The Ladies Monthly Magazine* littered across the floor testified to her attempt to divert her thoughts from Duncan Ramsey and the lonely years that stretched ahead of her. But these diversions had proved futile as had Cook's numerous attempts. All infusions and incantations had failed to raise Tina's spirits, and although Mr. Cadwallader, waiting in the library, had insisted that Cook inform her mistress of his desire to see her, Cook did not think she could budge Tina from her self-imposed exile.

Cook's assumption was correct.

"I don't wish to see anyone," Tina said for the third time in as many minutes. "Can't he leave a message?"

"Under the weather I told him ye were, but he says this bit of news is bound to be perking ye up. And says Mr. Cadwallader, he'll not be leaving until he can deliver it to no one but yerself, my lady."

Distractedly, Tina passed a hand over her eyes.

"Now missy, ye'll not be languishing about as if yer world had come to an end, not if I can be helping it."

Tina's head snapped up, her eyes opened. Cook had not called her missy since she was a very young girl, and although she did not like the old woman's stern voice, it was nonetheless comforting.

"There'll be no hiding the truth from yer old Cook. I'm knowing there's not a thing wrong with yer body. 'Tis yer heart that aches, and I'm also knowing that whatever's ailing yer heart is to be set upon the earl's platter. But I'll be wondering, what did that nice gentleman do that could be so terrible?"

"It's not what he did, but what I did. I fell in love with him."

"And that's bad?"

"Yes, when the gentleman is already betrothed to another lady."

"That's impossible." She clucked her tongue in disbelief. "Baked a groaning cake and buried it in hallowed ground. Even doctored his cocoa with a wee spot of briony root."

"Oh, Cook, you didn't."

"Indeed, I did. Hobbins and I agreed it was high time for ye to be falling in love and marrying, and the earl was our choice." Again she made that clucking noise as she scratched her head. "Can't imagine what went wrong. He was supposed to fall in love with ye, and ye were supposed to fall in love with him."

Tina gave a mirthless laugh. "And so he did, Cook, but that doesn't change the fact that he wasn't free to fall in love with anyone."

"Well, ye seem to have made a tidy package of logic out of all this. If 'tis all so clear to ye, then why are ye moping about? Ought to be putting some color in yer cheeks, missy, and getting on with the day-to-day business of living. And ye'll be starting by coming downstairs to see what it is that Mr. Cadwallader is wanting to tell ye."

"Very well," she replied without much enthusiasm. "I'll be down momentarily." Five minutes later, after combing her hair and pinning a brooch to the bodice of her dress, Tina proceeded to the library.

"Sir, how good of you to call," she said in an overbright voice.

Mr. Cadwallader rose from his seat by the

window. "And how good it is to see you, my lady. I apologize for my untimely intrusion, but I've received some news of particular interest, and I left my warehouse to bring it to you myself."

"Is it regarding the Council?"

"Yes, and I'm certain you'll concur the news is splendid. I had another visit from Silas Barnaby, and this time, he was not so threatening or cocksure of himself. Indeed, the wind was quite thoroughly emptied from his sails. It seems that the way the Council had managed to get a magistrate to consider eviction procedures was by collecting funds from the members and then offering a sizable gift to the magistrate."

"Do you mean a bribe?"

"Barnaby preferred to call it a gratuity."

"By any name, that's horrid."

"It is the way the system operates, I'm told."

"I see. Well, the good news, I suppose, is the magistrate refused to accept it."

"Not exactly. It seems someone else offered the magistrate another gift — one that was three times larger — not to consider the Council's petition, and the magistrate accepted it. Naturally, Barnaby is furious, for it appears the fellow had already taken the Council's money and refused to give it back."

Tina could not help laughing. "It serves them right for stooping to so low a tactic in the first place. Is this the end of it then?"

"I believe so. I'm told that the other members of the Council are so upset about the loss of their monies that they're disbanding the group."

"There's no Council anymore, not at all?" It sounded too good to be true.

"That's correct, and no rules or threats of any kind. And all owing to such a brilliantly simple solution. Can't imagine why I didn't think to try it myself."

Cook returned with a tea tray, and Tina said to her, "Mr. Cadwallader has brought news of a most splendid development. Our troubles with the Council are over for good."

"And what miracles have ye been accomplishing, Mr. Cadwallader?"

"Not I, Cook, but an anonymous sponsor. Just today I learned that someone offered the magistrate a gift to disregard the Council's charges, and the Council, having lost their funds, has decided to disband."

"An anonymous gift, ye say. A great deal of money, was it?"

"I'd say. Lady Christina's savior must be mighty powerful."

"Or much besotted by the sting of love," suggested Cook, looking like the cat who had managed to get to the bowl of cream.

Tina shot a warning glance at the old woman. She knew what Cook was thinking; she was thinking that the earl was responsible, and she was probably right.

Mr. Cadwallader remarked, "Hadn't thought of it like that. Must be one of your admirers, Lady Christina. Which one do you suppose it might be?"

"I haven't the vaguest clue, and besides, it doesn't matter, does it? The incident is over and done with, and that's what counts," Tina said, all the while knowing the identity of her savior was not something she could dismiss. In reality, it made all the difference in the universe to know that Duncan Ramsey had not been able to walk away from Cockleshell Manse and forget her. He might have gone out of her life forever, but he had not been able to erase her from his mind, and therein lay a troublesome paradox. On the one hand, the notion provided Tina with a curious sort of comfort; it conjured up an image of a guardian angel always waiting in the shadows to come to her rescue. On the other hand, it reminded her of how truly alone she was, how final their separation was, and how empty the days and years ahead of her were destined to be.

It was well past eleven o'clock in the evening, the hour when Hobbins normally made his final check around the premises to satisfy himself the doors and windows were secured, and the fires damped for the night. But tonight, lights were blazing in Cockle-shell Manse. Everyone, save the youngest children, was gathered in the library, and everyone was talking at once.

"Are you certain there wasn't a letter in her room?" Tina asked the upstairs maid. "You checked high and low?"

"Nothing, my lady."

"And all of her things are packed up and gone?" she asked Cook, who replied with an affirmative nod.

"Well, then, who was the last to see her?"

Lettie stepped forward.

"When was that?"

"Just before tea, Tina mum."

"And did she say where she was going?"

"No, she didn't."

"Did she say or do anything unusual?"

"Not unusual for her."

"And what did she do after tea?"

"Went up to her room, I think."

"That was the last you saw of her?"

"Yes, Tina mum."

"Was that the last anyone saw of her?" Tina looked at the faces around her as they each replied with a nod. No one had seen her since teatime. The unpredictable Miss Penny, it appeared, had run away from Cockleshell Manse.

"I don't understand what we did wrong," said Tina with remorse.

"Mayhap she saw a relative or friend of the family among your recent callers," suggested Hobbins.

"I had not thought of that. Well, whatever the reason, we can't allow her to roam the streets alone. We must find her and bring her back. Oh, dear, I knew it was wrong to let her stay without telling the whole truth, and now I shall be to blame if anything happens to her."

"Summon the earl is what ye must be doing," said Cook, who had been waiting for the first legitimate opportunity to force the gentleman to return to Cockleshell Manse.

"Is that necessary?" Reluctance was heavy in Tina's voice. While she admitted to the inevitability of one day encountering Duncan Ramsey she had not imagined it would be so soon. Somehow she imagined she would have had time to recover from the shock and hurt and sense of betrayal. She was not prepared to see him again. Her feelings for him remained strong, and her vulnerability was painfully open. How she would survive an interview with Ramsey, she did not know. "Why not summon Mr. Cadwallader instead? He might be able to get his dockworkers to form a search party."

"That's an excellent idea," agreed Hobbins.

"But ye'll be needing the help and advice of the earl as well. 'Tis high time for ye to be spreading word about the girl through the clubs, and 'tis no one better suited than the earl to be accomplishing that for ye."

Hobbins, seeing the wisdom of his wife's suggestion, amplified, "Indeed, the earl has government connections, and he could get word to the Runners and the local constabularies to be on the lookout for Miss Penny."

"Aye, calling the earl 'tis what ye must be doing right away, my lady. Bakerby," Cook said, turning to the footman, "Lady Christina will pen a letter to his lordship, and ye'll be delivering it to his rooms this very night."

Eleven

It was dawn when the earl, fagged and beginning to feel the stirrings of a monumental headache, returned to his rooms on Curzon Street. He had passed the night in the company of Ned and two unremarkable demi-reps at the Pigeon Hole. These past days, devoting his time to the green baize, French brandy, and easy women seemed a fine way to drown his conscience and erase the memory of Lady Christina's ashen face when she had bid him *au revoir*. A fine notion, mayhap, but hardly successful, for it was impossible to forget the pain that had reflected from the depths of those glorious lilac eyes. Unsuccessful, for in the end, he had to return to Curzon Street, where the silence was damning, and in the solitude of those rooms his guilt festered. Even the knowledge that he had managed to neutralize the Council did not blunt his shame. There was nothing he could do to repair the damage he had inflicted upon the most honorable lady he had ever known. His blind selfishness had ruined everything, and it was an awful burden, rather than precious memories, that he would carry for the remainder of his days.

This morning, he was surprised to see a weary-eyed footman hunkered up in his doorway. "Bakerby?" The young servant looked as if he had been waiting all night, and Ramsey's first thought was that something unspeakable had happened to Lady Christina or one of the children. "Bakerby, is that you?"

"Aye, my lord."

"What's wrong?" he inquired, a touch of panic ringing in his voice.

"Got a letter from her ladyship. Believe it explains everything, my lord."

As Ramsey opened the envelope he motioned for the footman to follow him through the doorway. Quickly, he perused the missive. It was brief and to the point.

Dear Lord Ramsey,

Due to unforeseen circumstances your presence is required at Cockleshell Manse as soon as possible. I fear for the safety of our guest, Miss Penny, who has disappeared, and I hope that you will agree to assist us in our search for her before it is too late.

Thank you ahead of time for your for-

248

bearance and assistance.

Your cousin, Christina Braughton.

Ramsey digested this intelligence with a mingling of relief and disappointment. It was good to learn that neither Lady Christina nor one of the children was ill or injured in any way, but he was disappointed that it was such an impersonal request. Ah, well, what was he to expect? A shower of effusive greetings and well-wishes? Hardly. Although she could not want to see him any more than he wished to see her, there was no choice but for him to go to Cockleshell Manse and offer whatever aid he could.

"Tell your mistress I shall arrive by nine o'clock," he said, calculating that it would require the better part of the next two hours to mend the damage done to his person by a long succession of endless nights and the regular overconsumption of alcohol.

"Aye, my lord." Bakerby bowed and departed.

True to his word, Ramsey rapped the tip of his cane upon the door of Cockleshell Manse as distant bells could be heard to toll nine times. It seemed like an eternity before anyone responded to his knock, and impatiently, Ramsey tweaked the right cuff of his white shirt, then straightened his waistcoat. For a gentleman who normally placed scant value on the dictates of fashion, he had chosen this outfit with unusual care. A new-fangled frock coat of the deepest royal blue and military in design defined his broad shoulders, and a pair of pale yellow pantaloons clung snugly to his muscular legs.

At last, Bakerby opened the door and directed the earl to the conservatory from which the trickle of water in the fish pond and the cries of Black Jack and the cockatoo echoed, and where Lady Christina awaited him. On the threshold of the two-storied glass structure, Ramsey stopped and stared across the room. Beneath a canopy of flowering orange trees, Lady Christina was seated upon a wicker longue. She did not see him, and for several moments, he studied the scene as if committing every detail to memory.

Reclining upon the longue, her dainty feet encased in Grecian sandals and peeping from beneath the hem of a simple sprigged muslin gown, she looked like the subject of a French painting. Morning sun bathed her, adding golden highlights to the abundant halo of sherry-colored hair that tumbled about her face, and enhancing the natural tint upon her delicate cheeks. The baby Diana was seated within the crook of her arm, chortling merrily and inspecting the silk flowers upon the brim of the lady's chip bonnet. Lady Christina demonstrated how to place the hat upon one's head, the child laughed, and then the lady said something, and although Ramsey could not hear her words, he knew they were gentle and kind, for the child rose upon chubby knees to hug Lady Christina.

How beautiful and rare the lady was as she pressed her lips to the babe's forehead. Love was written all across her face, and he could not help wondering if she had any love for him. An ache rose in his throat. He had been a fool to deny that he wished to see her; verily, he wished to do much more. For a moment, the urge to cross the room and take her in his arms was overwhelming, but he could not. He must never touch her again or allow himself to look upon her as anyone other than a concerned older relative.

There was a movement behind him in the corridor, and he turned to see Cook bustling toward the conservatory. She made a clucking noise with her tongue, and reaching his side, she whispered for his ears alone, "Ought to be taking a switch to ye, yer lordship, but for her sake I'll only be saying that ye'd better be behaving yerself this day."

Ramsey had thought there was nothing the old woman could say that would shock him, but obviously he had been misguided. Flabbergasted by this latest blunt and castigating remark, he merely nodded.

Taking no notice, Cook thrust out one bony hand and propelled him over the threshold. "And don't be standing there like a dumb-struck lad." Her voice rose. "Look who's here, my lady. 'Tis Lord Ramsey come to help with yer dilemma."

The lady looked up. The glow faded from her face, her pretty smile vanished, and again, there was a lump in Ramsey's throat at the thought of how much he had lost, how much he had destroyed.

The control he held over his emotions was tenuous at best, and carefully, he modulated his voice. "Good morning, Lady Christina," he said, sounding civil and wholly dispassion-ate. He executed an exquisitely formal bow.

Despite its distance his voice made Tina tremble. This interview was going to be much harder than she had imagined it might be. "Good morning, my lord," she said, immedi-ately diverting her regard back to the child and bonnet.

His jaw muscles clenched erratically, and deep lines flared out from his suddenly hard-ened mouth, but Tina did not see this, for she kept her own eyes resolutely fixed upon Diana.

"You are well?" he asked.

"Yes."

"And the children?" He allowed his gaze to wander toward the sound of their voices. They were outside on the lawn playing what appeared to be a game of blindman's buff. What had she told them about his departure? Did they miss him? Didn't they wonder why he had ceased to call upon them? No doubt she had told them the whole truth, and that being the case, it was unlikely they missed him one iota. It was much more probable that they held him in the lowest regard.

"The children are fine," Tina replied, raising her head a notch to peek at Ramsey's profile. In that instant, all that dwelled within her heart was reflected in her eyes. How handsome he looked. How tall and straight and strong. And how remote. Oh, why did it have to be this way? Why did they have to meet like this and behave like polite strangers? She took a deep steadying breath, and by the time he glanced in her direction again she had had time to regain control of her emotions and to pin a blandly polite smile upon her face.

"That's good," he said with a frown. The effort behind her polite smile was not lost on Ramsey. He knew how she was feeling, for her thoughts, her pain, and her struggles were his own. It was a dreadful situation, and he had to force himself to walk three steps closer to the wicker longue.

Diana extended her chubby arms to Ramsey, and he picked her up, thankful that he could focus upon the babe and not Tina. Diana patted his face and chortled, and Ramsey forced down another humiliating lump that was rising in his throat.

"And how are you, my sweet?" he inquired, hearing with shock the unsteady quality in his voice. He hardly sounded like himself at all. He hardly felt like himself. Lady Christina's soft voice drew his attention from Diana.

"I know it must have surprised you when Bakerby arrived with my note." She fidgeted with the silk ribband that was laced between the flowers on the bonnet. "I would not intrude upon your privacy under normal circumstances, but we're in quite a predicament with Miss Penny."

"So I gather." He shifted Diana from one arm to the other. "How may I help?"

"Ye can start by sitting down before ye drop that babe." Again Cook gave him a forceful prod forward, and he had no choice save to sit upon the edge of the longue, nearly landing upon Lady Christina's toes.

The lady blushed. "Have you had breakfast, sir?" She motioned to a wicker cart upon which a platter of pastries, several pots of jams, and a pitcher of milk rested.

"And even if he did, another bite never hurt a body," said Cook as she set a scone upon a plate along with a giant dollop of black currant preserve. She shoved the plate at the earl.

"I never eat in the morning," he stammered, wondering if the old woman had decided to cast a spell on him.

Again a flush of color rose upon Tina's cheeks. Poor man. Undoubtedly, he thought Cook was set on exacting some variety of vengeance with a fatal dash of hemlock. She took the proferred pastry, broke off a bite, and popped it in her mouth.

"Thank you, Cook. I'm sure if the earl wishes a pastry he will help himself." She set aside the plate, took Diana from Ramsey, and handed her to Cook. "Please take Diana to the nursery."

"Yes, my lady." And knowing she had been dismissed, Cook left the conservatory with the babe, but not before she had muttered to herself, "Periwinkle leaves and golden bees, Love between them find a home," three times for good luck.

"So Miss Penny has disappeared," Ramsey remarked as he moved from the end of the longue to a nearby chair.

"Yes," Tina responded, her eyes steadfastly focused upon the chip bonnet. "And given that Molly has more common sense than she does, I've no doubt the girl will manage to land herself in dire circumstances, if she hasn't already been kidnapped and shipped off to some pasha's harem." Faltering, she gave the silk ribband another tweak. "Miss Penny was my responsibility, and I feel terrible about this. I should have endeavored harder to get the truth from her, and now I don't know the first thing about how one goes about locating a wayward young lady."

"Don't worry. I shall handle all the details. We'll contact the Runners, notify all inns on roads leading out of town, and we should enlist Mr. Cadwallader's help to search the waterfront. You must, however, describe her to me once more."

"She's of medium height." Her gaze wandered from the bonnet to the fish pond, then to Black Jack as he soared overhead. "Her hair is light brown as are her eyes, and she's neither thin nor particularly full figured."

"Hmm. Sounds rather average. Is there nothing about Miss Penny that might distinguish her in a crowd?"

"She's probably wearing poppy pink."

"Poppy pink," he repeated as if discussing an outbreak of the most loathsome plague.

Tina felt his eyes touching her face, and she smiled. Involuntarily, she looked up, their eyes met and fused, and for one long loaded moment, he stared at her as if seeing into the depths of her soul. It was the kind of look that made her heart swim, a disturbing expression that was part wistfulness, part passion, and part despair. Then it was gone, a hooded look descended over his countenance, and she was persuaded that it had been nothing more than a trick of the early morning light.

She found her voice. "Yes, Miss Penny always vowed she would wear poppy pink when she encountered her true love, and that's what all of this running away was about in the first place. You see, her brother forced her into a betrothal with a gentleman she did not love, and then, having enlisted the counsel of a gypsy, she was convinced of the necessity of fleeing home to embark upon a search for her true love."

"And she's found him!" a third voice declared.

Tina and Ramsey turned toward the unexpected voice and saw the Countess of Brierly waving a piece of paper overhead as she entered the conservatory. "Received this letter just this morning, and came as soon as I could. It's from my brother Michael. He's eloped with Miss Penny."

"Thank goodness she's safe," said Tina.

"Though why they did not tell us of their

plans is peculiar." A frown creased the countess's brow. "I'm sorry Michael didn't confide in me. After all, he did have time to apply for a special license."

"Don't take it to heart. Perhaps the moon wasn't in its proper stage. There's no predicting with Miss Penny."

"Poor Michael," said the earl. "Your brother has my profoundest sympathies."

"I demand to know the meaning of this!" A bellicose voice came from behind them. Ramsey, Tina, and the countess looked at the doorway. In stalked Lord Tweeddale, his chest puffed out with self-importance, his face awash in the colors of anger.

"Lord Tweeddale," the ladies said in surprise. They each wondered what possible business he might have with either of them, and what it was that could possibly have put him into such a lather.

"Not now, Ned." Ramsey waved his hand toward the exit in a dismissive gesture.

"My business ain't with you, Ramsey." His lordship faced the countess. "I called at Berkeley Square to see you, ma'am, and was informed you were here."

"You were looking for me, sir?"

"Yes, indeed." He sneezed. "I was walking home at daybreak and saw my sister riding off in a carriage with one of your brothers."

"That's impossible. Kevin is in Ireland, and Michael is with his sweetheart, Miss Jane Penny. He's obtained a special license, and my guess is they intend to be married this day."

"Married!" His lordship's eyes bulged. "Whatever she might call herself, the gel I saw was Penelope — who, special license or no, is not of age — and *you*," he said, pointing a finger at Ramsey, "ought to be going after them!"

"If it really was your sister and my brother, why not you?" inquired the countess. "You are her guardian, are you not?"

"True, but *he's* betrothed to Penelope."

"What? Of late, I'd thought the earl and — " The unfinished sentence hung in the air as the countess regarded Ramsey, who was looking more uncomfortable by the moment, and then Lady Christina, whose cheeks were flying flags of fiery carmine. She turned back to the earl. "This is most perplexing, sir. What have you to say for yourself? Shame on you. Did you not know the whereabouts of your betrothed?"

"Indeed, I did, or at least I thought so. Ned told me she'd gone to visit her governess in Aylesbury." A sober look settled upon his countenance. "I say, Ned, you never told me Penelope was opposed to the betrothal."

"And what if she was?" Another round of sneezes beset Lord Tweeddale, and he cast a disparaging eye upon a nearby gardenia in full bloom. "It's a girl's duty to marry as her family sees fit, and you were my choice."

"That's despicable," said Tina, her eyes growing moist as the meaning of this unexpected development began to clarify amid the confusion. If Miss Penny was really Miss Latham, and if Miss Latham was the earl's affianced, but did not wish to marry him, then perhaps, if the earl had not experienced a change of heart, there was hope for her in that quarter. Suddenly, at the prospect of seeing Ramsey seated at the opposite end of the dining room table once again, and of being held in those muscular arms while he kissed her until she thought she would melt, her heart began to race.

"Despicable?" Lord Tweeddale gave a petulant shrug. "You are entitled to your opinion, my lady, but as far as I'm concerned the agreement with Ramsey still stands, and we must stop Penelope and O'Kieffe before it's too late."

"Have you the slightest inkling of all the damage you've done?" Ramsey, appalled at the notion of forcing his hand upon a young lady, demanded of his lordship. "Matters would have been a whole lot simpler if you'd only asked for a loan."

"Cut line, Ramsey. You've got no right to make yourself out to be lily-white in all of this." He pierced the earl with a leer and let his gaze travel from Ramsey to meaningfully rest upon Lady Christina. "If I don't miss the mark, I'd say you've been playing fast and — "

"Don't say another word, Ned. Not if you value your life," Ramsey ground out through clenched teeth. The loathing in his voice was as raw as it was menacing. "I always did say the lowliest creature was one who bartered his own flesh and blood to line his pockets."

For the first time in his adult life, Lord Tweeddale squirmed beneath the censorious regard of three pairs of eyes.

"If greed was Lord Tweeddale's motivation, then there's no reason to stop our siblings, for my brother has oodles more blunt than Ramsey," said the countess, sarcasm dripping from every syllable.

"But if Miss Latham is not of age, will the marriage be legal?"

"Given that Michael managed to obtain the license, I believe so. And while it might be illegal to perform such a ceremony, once done, the deed is legally binding." She faced his lordship. "Truth to tell, you should be thrilled that your sister displayed the pecuniary judgment to run off with Michael. Why, matters could have been immensely worse," she concluded, amusement warming her visage. "Just imagine if Madame Zaborini's fair-haired twin had been an actor or farmer."

The thought was an amusing one, and Tina could not help laughing. "But we should not let them marry without family and friends," she added as if all had agreed that the wedding of Miss Latham and Mr. O'Kieffe should take place. "This should be a day of memories they will always treasure, and they should wed with the knowledge their union is blessed."

The countess agreed, and when Lord Tweeddale opened his mouth to offer further objection, the earl silenced him.

Tina wished the earl would glance her way so she might measure his reaction to these developments. Was his heart racing like hers? And as she had done, had he experienced the sudden lifting of a great weight from his shoulders? But he looked everywhere else except at her, and save for the loathing he showed Lord Tweeddale his mood was unreadable. There was no way to surmise his thoughts, and Tina faced the countess. "Where might they be bound?"

"I'm sure they're headed for Thornhill Park — our mother's ancestral seat in Kent. Mama was wed there in the estate's chapel, it's where we were raised, and Michael always vowed to marry there."

"Then to Kent we must be bound. Is there time?"

"We can't be but a few hours behind them, and if we miss the ceremony, we shall at least be able to wish them well, for I'm certain our nurse Nanny Saltmarsh will descend upon them and make them spend their wedding night in the Queen's Chamber at the Park. It's been the practice for several generations, and Nanny Saltmarsh would never let anyone deviate from tradition."

Thus it was that a veritable caravan set forth from London southward bound on the Dover road for Thornhill Park. In the first carriage rode the countess, Tina, and the girls, who had been dressed in matching frocks and could hardly contain their excitement at the prospect of being party to an elopement; Ramsey and the three boys traveled in the second carriage; in the third vehicle was a sneezing Lord Tweeddale, who had been assigned the care of Prince Charlie, Robert Bruce, and a score of floral arrangements from the conservatory to decorate the hoped-for wedding celebration.

It was late afternoon when they turned off the open road and proceeded down an avenue of oaks to Thornhill Park. At the end of the drive there were two vehicles parked before the Tudor manor house.

Lord Tweeddale leapt from the stuffy confines of his carriage. "There's O'Kieffe's phaeton!" he shouted, sneezing and pointing to the more expensive of the two rigs.

"And I believe the other carriage belongs to the parson," the countess said as she and Tina alighted from their barouche. The boys, liberated spaniels yapping at their heels, were already dashing up the steps and into the house as if it were their own, and the girls, having each taken an armful of flowers from Lord Tweeddale's vehicle, hurried after them. At a more sedate but definitely anxious pace, the countess led Tina, Ramsey, and Lord Tweeddale into her childhood home. "Come this way. To the chapel." She motioned to the children, and the entire entourage proceeded down a narrow paneled corridor.

At the end of the hallway was an ornately carved door about which the walls were painted in imitation of medieval tapestries. The door was ajar, and the children burst through followed by the adults. Their arrival was not a silent one, and the first voice to rise above the din of children and dogs, shuffling crinolines, and scraping boots was Penelope's.

"Sweet Jupiter," she screamed upon seeing

her brother and the earl enter the chapel. In highly dramatic fashion, she leaned on Mr. O'Kieffe as if on the verge of a swoon, and she clutched at her bosom with one trembling hand. "All is lost, dearest Michael, we've been betrayed, and it's to be as I told you it would. My brother shall separate us until we meet again in eternity."

For a moment there was silence, then everyone began talking at once.

"Look again, sweetling," Mr. O'Kieffe said to Penelope. "Though I know not their purpose, it doesn't appear my sister or the earl or your brother arrive in anger."

"You wicked boy," exclaimed the countess, running forward to hug her brother and the much befuddled Penelope. "Our only anger was that you did not confide in us."

"I don't understand," said Penelope, inching behind Mr. O'Kieffe as her brother took a step toward them.

"Oh, Miss Penny, I mean Miss Latham," began Tina. "If only you had told the truth as I asked when you first arrived at Cockleshell Manse, none of this would have happened."

"It wouldn't?" Her distressed gaze flitted between the earl and her brother.

"No, it wouldn't, and you would have saved those who care about you much worry. Indeed, had you been truthful with the earl and told him of your feelings about the betrothal, you never would have needed to consult Madame Zaborini nor place yourself in jeopardy by running away."

Penelope regarded Ramsey. "You would have understood, my lord?"

"Of course. I'm not an ogre, Miss Latham, and would never have forced myself upon an unwilling bride."

"But Ned said you were — "

"Your brother thought of no one save himself, and though I, too, must own some of the blame for not seeking to understand your sensibilities that is all in the past, and I trust you will accept my felicitations upon this happy occasion."

"That's why you're here? You're not here to take me home?" Penelope searched their faces, her gaze resting at last upon her brother's countenance.

Everyone waited for Lord Tweeddale to speak.

His lordship sneezed, and thrusting one of the damnable bouquets toward his sister, he said, "Yes, we came to wish you luck and to stand witness."

"Ah, then there's to be a wedding after all?" inquired the parson, who was not as perturbed as one might assume by this peculiar twist of events. The reputation of the O'Kieffe brothers was well known in the neighborhood, and it would have been highly out of character for an O'Kieffe and most boring for the local tabbies, if the parson returned home with nothing more to report than a mere elopement. "And who will give away the bride?"

The earl turned to Lord Tweeddale. "I would like that honor, Ned, if you don't mind."

His lordship tossed his hands in the air. "As there's nothing in the least bit proper about any of this, I don't see why not."

And so it was that the Honorable Penelope Latham became Mrs. Michael O'Kieffe. Afterward the impromptu wedding party spilled forth onto the garden terrace to dine upon a hastily prepared collation of cold salmon with a variety of festive edibles, imbibe the finest champagne, and enjoy the view of the rolling countryside at twilight.

"As long as we're being unconventional, I would like to offer a toast to my brother and his bride," the countess said, raising a fluted champagne glass. "To true love — may it always triumph."

The groom, seated between his sister and Penelope, leaned toward the countess to give her a kiss. "Perhaps it is unconventional for a lady to make a toast, but your sentiments, dear sister, are certainly not out of character. May true love triumph!"

The toast resounded about the table.

Tina took a sip of the sparkling wine and peered over the edge of the glass at the happiness surrounding her. The smile touching her lips spread to her eyes as the children echoed their own boisterous salutations to which the countess and the bride and groom replied, and even Lord Tweeddale managed a toast wishing the fruits of good fortune upon the couple. Then her regard fell upon Duncan Ramsey. He was seated opposite her, and heat rose in her cheeks as he raised his glass and mouthed the words, *To true love.*

It was a bold action on his part, throwing Tina into a state of discomposure. She had never been flirted with in such an outrageous fashion, and she could not help wondering whether it was nothing more than flirtatiousness prompted by the spirit of the moment. Should she act the lady to the hilt and rebuff him, or should she return his wicked grin with a playful one of her own? In her heart she wished to play along with whatever game he intended. There could be no harm in it — she had nothing to lose — and besides, the play might even reveal if there was any future for herself and this gentleman.

Quickly, before she might change her mind,

she rose from her seat and moved around the table until she stood beside him. "I, too, wish to be unconventional this day, my lord," she said in a soft voice. Her smile was surprisingly steady and decidedly mischievous. "Would you care to escort me on a tour of the grounds? I'm told the walk to the lake pavilion is lovely in the spring."

Pleasure, instant and glowing, sprang to the earl's eyes. "A sterling idea, my lady." He stood, set his linen serviette upon the table, and offered Tina his arm. His voice lowered an octave, and he whispered, "Has anyone told you how beautiful you are when you dare to be unconventional?"

Light tinkling laughter bubbled forth from Tina, and she slipped her arm in his as they started down the path to the lake. "They have not, my lord, but as a lady always appreciates flattery mayhap I should be unconventional on a more regular basis."

"You would, of course, choose your company with discretion?"

"Of course."

"And you would strive to prevent such behavior from becoming a habit?"

"Of course."

"Then I see no harm in it," he concluded. "But only on those occasions when it seems the most suitable course of action."

"Of course."

They lapsed into silence as they neared the end of the path. The field beyond the lake sloped gently upward and was blanketed in jonquils stretching from the water's edge to where sky met land, and the sun's final rays streaked across the water to wash the pavilion in the gold and purple hues of twilight. When they reached the lakeside structure, Ramsey freed Tina's arm and she walked across the tiled floor to a staircase that led into the lake. Folding her skirt about her, she sat on the top step and reached down to let her fingers churn the water.

"It was a jolly celebration, don't you agree?" Ramsey said, catching up with her.

"Yes, I think so, but as it's the only wedding I've ever been to I'm not the best one to judge."

Her words reminded him of the time she had told him the flowers from Cadwallader were her first, and as had happened then, something tightened about his chest. There was so much she had missed and so much more she deserved. How wrong he was to flirt with her instead of divulging what it was that lay in his heart. If he had learned anything these past weeks, it was that honesty was the only path to follow, and there was no time like the present. Crouching down beside Tina, he reached out to still the restless movement of her hand as it skimmed across the water's surface. The tight lines upon his face relaxed when she looked up at him and smiled.

"Perhaps the first, but hardly the last. I think you shall be attending another wedding celebration in the near future."

Tina's breath caught in her throat. Could he possibly mean what she hoped he did? She tilted her head sideways in question.

He clarified, "Yours and mine." There, it was said, and she had not shown him her back nor cried out in protest.

"You wish to marry me, sir?"

"Indeed, I do. There's an awful lot I have to make up for."

Her heart began to sink. "Is that the only reason?"

"No, it's not." Gently, he cupped her chin with those long, lean fingers, and holding her thusly, he stared into her eyes. His voice was hoarse. "You're the lady with whom I wish to spend my life."

She trembled slightly. "That's all?" Her tongue darted out to moisten her lips, and for a second, she closed her eyes. It had been exceedingly forward to suggest this walk; now she must be bold again. Her eyes opened to his ardent and encouraging gaze, and she dared to ask, "What of love? I could never marry a gentleman if there was not love between us."

He let out a boyish whoop of jubilation, taking her into his arms and pulling both of them to their feet. "Then your answer is yes? You'll marry me?"

"Only if you love me, my lord."

"Love you? What did you think this was all about? Of course, I love you," he said in a booming voice as if announcing it to the world.

"Then you must prove it," she replied with a saucy grin that set her lilac eyes twinkling. "Kiss me."

"I love you, sweet lady," he said, pulling Tina against his chest and punctuating each word with a series of light kisses. "I love you as no man has loved before or ever will."

"That's as it should be, my lord. And I love you," she whispered in a voice scratchy with emotion. Oh, it was wonderful to admit the truth that had been hidden and unspoken for so long. A laugh of gay abandon escaped her lips.

"And what's so amusing?"

"Oh, it's not you, but something the countess said to me weeks ago . . . something that's proven quite valid."

"What was that?"

"That one generally finds love in the most unexpected places."

"Ah, and I take that to mean I was unexpected."

She gave him a sassy smile and stood on tiptoe to kiss him. "Somewhat," she said, her lips continuing to brush his until he moaned in reply.

"Well, at least we know what to expect of the future. As I shall never leave your side, love will never evade us again." His mouth covered hers in a gentle, lingering caress. At last, he raised his head, blue eyes fusing with lilac. "I trust that meets with your approval?"

"Perfectly," came Tina's breathless response as that peculiar melting sensation began to seep through her limbs.

"Shall we return to the terrace to tell the others our good news?"

Tina's lips puckered into a tiny pout. "Must we go right away, my lord?"

A deep laugh rose from Ramsey's chest, and in reply his fingers threaded through soft sherry curls as he lowered his head to claim her lips in a searingly intimate kiss.

THORNDIKE-MAGNA hopes you have enjoyed this Large Print book. All our Large Print titles are designed for easy reading, and all our books are made to last. Other Thorndike Press or Magna Print books are available at your library, through selected bookstores, or directly from the publishers. For more information about current and upcoming titles, please call or mail your name and address to:

THORNDIKE PRESS
P.O. Box 159
Thorndike, Maine 04986
(800) 223-6121
(207) 948-2962 (in Maine and Canada call collect)

or in the United Kingdom:

MAGNA PRINT BOOKS
Long Preston, Near Skipton
North Yorkshire,
England BD23 4ND
(07294) 225

There is no obligation, of course.